DAMAGED

little girl

SUNNI T. CONNOR

DISCLAIMER

TO MY MOTHER

Thank you for allowing me to share our story. I say our story because my choice to expose my life resulted in your life challenges coming to the light as well. You stood by me throughout the entire process and allowed me to tell my story without shaming me for sharing OUR truth. For that, I love you more than words could ever express. You showed me love and affection my entire life. You believed in me and encouraged me to follow my dreams. Some chapters were challenging for you to read and even harder for you to deal with. I forcefully opened a lot of old baggage. I ripped the band-aid off many unhealed scars. I was blunt, honest, and raw about our life challenges. You are and will forever be my Queen. You are the light that brightens my day. I have no regrets, and I don't blame you for any of life's tests. We passed every test together, even when we "failed." This book was my closure to so much pain. Your support allowed the shackles to be removed from my heart, mind, and spirit. I am free now. We are free now. We are not our past, and we are not people's opinions. We are just us, and they are JUST PEOPLE. Mama, some may judge or even look at us differently, but we will accept the critique together and move forward with confidence. We have God, and family and no human will ever break us. God made you for me, and I happily accept the BEST MOTHER IN THE WORLD.

Love Sunni T

CONTENTS

CONTENTS CONTINUED

INTRODUCTION

Wow, you picked this book up, huh? Are you mentally prepared to be introduced to the life of a DAMAGED little girl? You will go through an emotional rollercoaster on this reading journey. You will vividly be a part of this damaged life, where you will have no choice but to grow through the eyes of Sunni.

If you are expecting an ordinary book, written in a traditional way, with an average plot and a typical conclusion, this is not that book. There is nothing normal about DAMAGED little girl, and I would hate to disappoint you. Then again, what is normal? If you have a vivid imagination, a heart, and a little tough skin, we will be a perfect fit together. You can achieve courage with me on this journey. Believe me, courage is something I required to survive this life.

As much as I would love to go on and on about why reading this book will change your outlook on life, I would prefer not. I say this with love, of course. If these three short, unconventional paragraphs have you intrigued at all, then buckle your mental seat belt, buy this book and come on a sick ride with me. You will enter my mind and experience my true life as a DAMAGED little girl. Come on, flip the page.

DAMAGED little girl

CHAPTER 1

THERE MUST BE A BEGINNING BEFORE AN END

Queen was beautiful and confident. She had smooth milk chocolate skin, full lips, and thick black hair that flowed down her back. In the '80s, skin complexion was a big deal. There was a lot of black-on-black racism. Imagine that! Some black people thought a lighter skin tone was better, or should I say, fair skin, as some like to call it. People often told Queen, "You are very beautiful to be dark." She always thought *you can take that compliment and shove it up your ass!* In her mind, it was more of an insult than a compliment. Why couldn't she just be beautiful? Queen didn't crave B.S. compliments or fake attention. Her confidence showed in everything she did. She walked boldly, talked proudly, and loved herself for who she was. The boys loved her, and the girls wanted to be around her. Queen had a vibrant personality filled with humor. She was desirable, spontaneous, and down to earth.

It was June 8, 1984, one of the hottest days of the year. Baltimore has the perfect four seasons; when it's winter, it's brutally cold; when it's summer, it's scorching hot. It rains the entire spring, and fall is mild and colorful. Queen was 16 years old with four sisters and two brothers. She was closest with her 17-year-old sister Shelby. Queen sat on her stoop with her big bamboo earrings, a thick gold choker chain, and a fresh pair of Reeboks tennis shoes while wearing a new pair of "USED" jeans.

"Do you have a light?" Queen asked.

"Yes. Give my lighter back too. You always keep my lighters," Shelby responded. She held her hand out, waiting for her lighter.

Queen lit up a fresh Newport cigarette. She took a long deep drag and asked, "Do you want something from the store?"

"No, I'm ok Sis," Shelby responded.

Queen walked to the corner store to get an ice-cold Pepsi. She awkwardly waved to one of the neighborhood guys she caught staring as she walked. Queen prayed he didn't try to talk game to her, although she was fully prepared to reject him. As she came out of the store with her head down, she bumped into a guy with a head full of curly hair, brown eyes, thick dark eyebrows, with light caramel skin.

"Excuse me, pretty lady," he said.

"No excuse me, Handsome," Queen said. She licked her lips and put her hand out to give him a formal shake.

"Handsome?" he asked. He blushed and reached out to shake her hand.

"Hi, I'm Queen, and you are?" she asked with fluttery eyes.

"I'm Desmond," he said. He smiled with the most prominent white teeth as he let go of her hand. They left the store and went their separate ways.

Desmond was 15 years old with four siblings. He lived five blocks away from Queen. Desmond's mother, Mrs. Pam, was a Jehovah's Witness. She strongly worshiped her Religion and believed full-heartedly. Although Desmond had four siblings, he mainly hung out with his older brother Charlie. Charlie had his own place. His apartment equaled freedom. Charlie was known in the neighborhood as the "Weed Man." He sold weed and worked a 9-5 job. Charlie was no stranger to the ladies; they recognized his dark skin, muscular physique, and confident personality. Charlie had his swag together. He wore a navy-blue Fila velour sweatsuit, with a fresh pair of new Fila sneakers to match. He went to his mother's house to approach Desmond.

"Desmond, when you were over my house, did you take my fresh pair of shell heads?" Charlie asked.

"You said I could wear them. I asked when you were on the phone," Desmond responded in an explanatory tone.

"I don't remember that, Desmond. Stop taking my shit when you come over," Charlie demanded.

They argued for a few minutes as siblings often do. Desmond and Charlie's arguments were intense. They yelled and screamed at each other to make their point, then they moved on as if nothing happened. That was their regular routine. They argued and let it go, which is why it was best to stay out of their fights. Desmond told Charlie about bumping into Queen.

"I've heard of Queen," Charlie stated arrogantly.

"Your old ass is played out. You don't know the fresh meat around here," Desmond said in a joking tone.

"Do you know who I am? Trust me, little brother, I can set you up," Charlie chuckled.

They were distracted by the strong aroma of fried chicken coming from the kitchen. Mrs. Pam asked if they were hungry, and they ran into the kitchen like hungry scavengers. The chicken was fresh out of the grease. Desmond hurriedly took a bite and burned his tongue from the chicken being too hot. Mrs. Pam fussed at him for not properly sitting at the table and eating with some class. Eating was love, and there is no greater love than a mother's cooking. The smell and feeling you get from eating your mother's home-cooked meals are irreplaceable.

It was the fall of 1985, and school just started. Desmond was walking down the school hallway when he first saw Queen again. She was breathtaking; he noticed her right away. She wore a tight stone-washed skirt, pink slouch socks, with an oversized pink and brown shirt. Queen hung around an older crowd. Her being with the slightly older teenagers didn't intimidate Desmond.

Everyone knew Desmond well in their neighborhood. The dudes knew not to play with him, and the ladies had their eyes on him. Light-skinned, pretty boys were in style, and Desmond was winning in the looks department. Weak or timid girls weren't Desmond's type. He desired a girl like Queen. His new goal became getting Queen to be his lady. He observed Queen's aggressive, strong personality, and it made him want her more. Desmond found himself more intrigued by Queen the more he looked at her. He thought, *what is it about her? Why am I tripping over this chick?* Just as the thought crossed his mind, Queen walked up to him.

"Desmond, right?" she asked with flirtatious eyes.

"Queen, right?" he rhetorically asked.

Desmond's best friend Braden walked up, interrupting their conversation.

"What's up, D Man? I didn't know you knew Queen," Braden stated.

"I had the pleasure of briefly meeting Queen a little while ago," Desmond responded. He looked at Queen with desire in his eyes.

Just as Desmond finished his sentence, Braden's little brother Stan walked up.

"What's going on?" Stan asked Desmond and Queen.

"What do you mean? What does it look like?" Desmond responded with aggression.

Stan liked Queen too. He didn't always see eye to eye with Desmond. Stan began to argue with Desmond, and before long, they were physically fighting. Queen was flattered at the thought of them fighting over her, but she assumed they already had issues. She was right. They didn't click, and they continually got into brawls. Queen had no interest in Stan; they went on one date, and she shortly realized there was no chemistry between them.

On the other hand, Queen and Desmond became great friends. Once they built a friendship, they were inseparable. The two were together every day from that day forward. Queen was older and more experienced. She had a massive influence over Desmond. It wasn't long before she had him smoking cigarettes, smoking weed, and doing pretty much whatever she said.

Charlie had a one-bedroom apartment which he turned into "The Party House." Desmond's best friend Braden was an awesome DJ, so he and Charlie collaborated on these amazing house parties. Together they rocked the house. Charlie charged $2 at the door, and he made his extra money off the weed he sold to the guest. These parties were fun and profitable. Desmond walked into the party with his Queen on his arm. Queen was flashy; she wore an all-red leather bodysuit, big bamboo earrings, and a pair of black heels. Her hair was in a freshly crimped style slicked to the side.

Desmond wore a pair of stone-washed jeans and a white shirt with Charlie's fresh pair of shell-head Adidas that he never returned. Queen invited her friend Janice to come along to the party. Braden had the music jumping, and everyone was dancing.

Janice walked over to Braden and asked, "Can you play Planet Rock by the Afrika Bambaataa & The Soul Sonic Force?"

"Why didn't you just say the name of the song?" Charlie asked as he chuckled.

"I don't know," she shyly responded and walked away.

"Come on, Janice, this our jam girl. Hi Charlieeeeee!" Queen yelled with excitement.

"What's up, Queen, and what's up with Janice? She's cute," Charlie asked while pulling Queen to the side away from the crowd.

"Go ask her! She's right there. She's definitely single, though." Queen pointed in Janice's direction to gesture that Charlie should make his move.

"Thanks for the heads up Sis," Charlie said to Queen as he went to approach Janice. They danced the night away, and in a matter of days, they became an official couple. All four of them hung out daily, brothers and best friends. It was the beginning of many fun nights they would all have together as couples.

One Sunday morning, Desmond's mother, Mrs. Pam, left to go to the kingdom hall to worship Jehovah. Mrs. Pam truly loved Queen; however, she was strict. No one was allowed in her house when she wasn't home. Nor did she affiliate herself with many people who weren't considered Jehovah Witness, but there was something about Queen that she loved. Queen happily invited herself over to Desmond's house. She knew

Mrs. Pam went to the kingdom hall every Sunday no matter what. She burst into Desmond's front door without knocking.

"Hey Desmond, I saw Mrs. Pam leave," Queen announced.

"Oh, that's what you saw, huh, Queen?" Desmond responded. He looked up at Queen out of shock.

"Are you ready for me, Desmond?" she boldly asked. She lightly pulled her bra strap over her shoulder.

He looked at her with a confused expression, but before he could respond, Queen grabbed his hands and pulled him down the basement steps. Queen knew something Desmond didn't know. She knew it was time to take their relationship to the next level. She wasted no time showing Desmond what she came over for on that early Sunday morning. Before she reached the third step, she had her shirt, pants, and socks off. She stood at the bottom of the steps and looked up at Desmond with her bright seductive eyes.

"I'm waiting for you to remove the rest," Queen implied in a naughty voice.

"Oh, I'm going to remove the rest," he said in an eager tone.

Desmond thought, *oh shit, it's about to go down*. Desmond was tough on the streets, but he was a virgin. He wanted to lose his virginity to Queen; he was comfortable with her. He was nervous as hell but tried his best not to show it.

"We really about to do this?" Desmond asked with hesitation.

"Yes," Queen nodded.

Desmond moved with aggression as he became more excited about what was about to happen.

In a low seductive voice, Queen whispered, "Slow, Desmond, slow,"

Desmond entered Queen's kingdom and savored every second of losing his virginity. Queen trained him on all her desires, and before long, they both released in ecstasy. They lay there and smoked a cigarette while sweating and breathing heavily from exhaustion. Queen had questions. Desmond seemed to know more than a virgin would know for it to be his first time.

"Are you sure this was your first time?" Queen asked in disbelief.

"Yeah, girl," he quickly answered.

"Ok, good, I don't want to have to fuck you up!" she shouted unexpectedly.

"Queen, you crazy girl!" he laughed. He rubbed her hair as their naked bodies lay closely in sweat and skin.

From that day forward, Desmond knew Queen's body like the back of his hand. She demanded his sexual attention every day, and we all know what that can lead to. Needless to say, 9 months later I would arrive! The SUN has shined. It's brighter than the usual morning horizon. A baby King was coming or not.

Queen and Desmond went to their 6th-month prenatal visit, and the doctor informed them they were having a baby boy. They were both excited, but Queen was secretly praying for a girl. Queen was extremely sick her entire pregnancy. She had to quit her job and change her entire way of living. No cigarettes, no Pepsi, and no fried foods. Everything she loved made her sick. The little human inside of her had a mind of its own and overpowered Queen's body. She literally ate fruit her entire pregnancy, and she couldn't even bear the smell of cigarettes, weed, or her father's famous fried fish. Close to the end of her pregnancy, she began to panic. She realized they didn't have everything for their new little bundle of joy. Desmond and Queen lay in his bed in a spoon position while watching TV.

"Desmond, the baby still needs a crib and a car seat. I'm getting worried. He will be here soon," Queen stated as she rubbed her stomach.

"Don't worry, baby. Our son will have everything he needs, I promise," he responded in a calm unbothered tone.

"Ok, but can we at least get the car seat this week?" she impatiently asked.

"Trust me, baby. He will come into this world right. Stop worrying," he assured her.

Desmond wasn't too sure how he would get all the things his son needed, but he knew he had to find a way. At the time, he worked for Gunther's Trash Company, but that wasn't enough money for his bills and all the things the baby needed. He was living on his own, renting a basement apartment from a friend.

Desmond built a relationship with Queen's brother Bubba. Bubba was an adventurer. He lived life exactly how he wanted, unapologetically. If he needed something, he took it. Once Desmond told him there were money issues, Bubba decided his Nephew would not be born into this world without his necessities. Bubba schooled Desmond on how to take what he needed without getting caught. Without a thought, Desmond followed Bubba's lead and took what he needed for his unborn child. A few days later, Desmond knocked on Queen's door with excitement. She opened the door and smiled. Desmond had a crib, car seat, walker, pampers, bottles, blankets, and a brand-new blue stroller.

"I knew you would make sure our baby boy came into this world the right way," Queen said as she gave Desmond a big hug.

"I told you, there is nothing I won't do for him. Our son will have everything he deserves," he stated. Desmond continued to bring more baby items into Queen's house.

"Yes, he will. He will be everything we dreamed he would be," Queen stated with a soft smile while admiring Desmond's ambition.

She watched him in silence as he continued to bring all the new items into her house. This moment reminded her of why she loved him so much.

It was March 1986, one of the windiest days in the history of Maryland. A precious little <u>girl</u> was born into a cruel world with every hope in her little cry of being a decent human being. The poor little girl couldn't understand what the future held for her. The doctor's smack wouldn't be the last smack her soft skin would feel from the cruelty of what life had planned for her.

Queen and Desmond returned home with a beautiful 6-ounce baby <u>girl</u> with a head full of dark straight hair. She looked just like Desmond, so much so, she was often mistaken for a beautiful little boy. The little boy they thought they were having turned out to be a girl. The doctors mistakenly told them the wrong gender. Queen's prayers worked; she got her little girl. They named her SUNNI. Queen's sister Shelby came up with the name. It was the best day of both of their lives.

Desmond felt there was nothing he wouldn't do to protect Sunni. The instant feeling of butterflies and love was like no feeling he'd ever experienced. Desmond seemed to be more excited that he had a girl instead of the boy he was expecting. Queen was just as much in love with Sunni. As time progressed, Queen realized she no longer wanted to invest her time in a committed relationship. Queen was young and vibrant. She went from doing her own thing to having a baby and a man to share her life with. One early morning, Desmond and Queen got into a heated argument while on the telephone.

"I don't want to do this anymore, and you can't see Sunni anymore either!" Queen yelled.

"Have you lost your mind? I will see my daughter whenever I want. Don't play with me, Queen!" Desmond screamed into the phone with anger.

Desmond couldn't believe what he'd just heard. He hung up the phone and called Charlie to tell him how Queen was tripping and how she talked about keeping Sunni from him. Charlie told him, Queen was just upset and would never take Sunni from him. Desmond told him she wouldn't get the chance because he was taking Sunni. He waited until the next day and took Sunni from her babysitter, who lived two doors down from Queen's house. When Queen got off work, she went to get Sunni but was told she had already left with her father. Queen had no choice but to pull out the big guns. She had to tell her father, Mr. Charles.

"Daddy, Desmond kidnapped Sunni, and he said he's not bringing her back," she cried.

"Don't cry, baby. It'll be ok. I'll get my granddaughter back. Where is Desmond now?" Mr. Charles asked.

"I don't know. He's not answering. I called his house so many times!" she screamed in a panicked voice.

Desmond took Sunni to the park for most of the day. He kept her away from his usual hangout spots. Desmond was actually running out of ideas for how to entertain a baby. Mr. Charles put the word out to everyone in the neighborhood to tell Desmond he was looking for him. Mr. Charles finally reached Desmond on the phone later that night.

"Now, Desmond, I love you like a son, but you better bring that girl back," he said in a calm but vicious tone.

"Mr. Charles, Queen was the one who-," he attempted to explain when Mr. Charles cut him off.

"Desmond, this is my only warning. You know I have that shotgun, and I love my girls. Now bring that baby back!" he spoke firmly without yelling.

Against Desmond's wishes, he returned Sunni to Queen. He knew not to play with Mr. Charles. Nor did he have a secret location to hold Sunni captive. Queen knew all his hangouts; he couldn't keep her at the park forever. Mr. Charles forced Desmond and Queen to have a conversation so they wouldn't involve him or Sunni in their drama again. They came to a mutual understanding to be friends but no longer pursue a relationship. They had one rule for co-parenting. The rule was simple; before either of them could bring Sunni around a new mate, the other parent had to meet them first. It was the beginning of a beautiful parenting relationship.

Queen flopped down on Shelby's bed with her 10-month-old baby. The old fan in the front room made an annoying screeching sound.

"Damn, Sunni looks just like Desmond. She could've at least got some of my chocolate complexion," Queen complained.

"Desmond spit her out. You had nothing to do with that baby," Shelby agreed.

"I know, right. It doesn't make any sense. I carry this fat heavy baby around every day who looks nothing like me," Queen laughed. "You know you are my favorite sister, right?"

"What do you want now, Queen?" she asked in an anxious voice.

"Can Sunni stay with you again? It's this dope party I want to go to. I'll be back before breakfast," she begged.

"Breakfast? Are you crazy? Nope, Nope, Nope. I watched her for the last two nights," Shelby reminded Queen. She shook her head and picked up a shirt off the floor.

"Please, Sis. I will bring you some money, and I won't ask for at least a week," she begged.

Shelby finally agreed after Queen made many persuasive attempts. She took Sunni out of Queen's arm and laid her on her chest, rocking her back and forth while singing "What Have You Done for Me Lately" by Janet Jackson. Queen gave her sister a big hug and started singing while looking for something to wear out on the town. Shelby was quiet and the complete opposite of Queen. She was a homebody. She loved staying in with the kids. Shelby had two kids of her own by the time Sunni was born. Diamond and Darin. Might as well make that three kids, the way she took Sunni under her wing. That was her niece, and their bond was strong from the very beginning. Although she had her own two young kids, she adored Sunni.

When Sunni was one, she had a bad asthma attack. No one in Queen's family had asthma, so no one knew how to help her. Her grandmother Mrs. Pam (Desmond's mother), had terrible asthma. Queen picked up the rotary phone with urgency and called Mrs. Pam.

"It's happening again! Should I take her back to the hospital?" Queen hollered.

"Calm down, Queen. Catch a cab, and I'll take care of my baby. We don't need no doctors for what I know how to do," Mrs. Pam responded with calmness.

Whenever Sunni had an asthma attack, Mrs. Pam would care for her. Mrs. Pam loved Sunni more than words could ever describe. She initially wasn't happy that Desmond was having a baby so young. Mrs. Pam also felt Desmond was breaking Jehovah's beliefs. All those feelings left the day she laid eyes on Sunni. Mrs. Pam felt the joy of having Desmond all over again. She enjoyed taking her to the Kingdom Hall and dressing her up to praise Jehovah. Although Queen was not a Jehovah's Witness, she never interfered with Mrs. Pam taking Sunni to the Kingdom Hall.

Tom was Desmond's baby brother, Mrs. Pam's youngest child. Tom loved Sunni so much. He was only eight years old when she was born. Finally, he felt like he wasn't the baby in the house anymore. Tom carried Sunni everywhere as if she was his new toy. He was a proud little uncle. The entire house fought over her attention, including her two aunts. She got the same love from her aunts and uncles on Queen's side of the family. Sunni was born into an abundant amount of love. She started her life surrounded by love and joy from both sides of her family. Sadly, for Sunni, things would be changing quickly. All this love and Joy would soon come to an end.

CHAPTER 2

MEET SUNNI & THE DEVIL

I'm Sunni, and I'm filled with hope and ambition. I'm the spitting image of my father. I'm fair-skinned with bright eyes, and long lashes; I have a nice grain of dark brown hair and a slim physique. I see the best in everything and everyone, that is until life showed me the worst. I'm an innocent, naive, sensitive, emotional, talkative, dramatic little girl. Life is pretty good at this stage. Sadly, this phase of my life will drastically change at only the age of four. If only I could hold on to these happy moments a little longer before the Devil comes for me. He patiently waits and strategically hides in the shadows for the perfect opportunity to take my innocence. Before we give the Devil too much attention as we often do in life, let's rewind back to the age of two before I met the Devil.

Here we go. This was my first death experience, but for sure wouldn't be the last. At just two years old, I lost my grandmother to breast cancer. Although I was only two, I would never experience or have that kind of love again. The same day she died, her house burned down. My aunts and uncles lost their mother and their home all on the same day. I always yearned for a grandmother. My grandmother on my mother's side died before I was born, and I had lost the only other grandmother I could ever have.

I always wanted to lay on my grandmother's breast, smell her neck, and cry about how life completely fucked me over. I wanted to go into the kitchen and smell fresh collard greens cooking and think to myself, *"I'm at my granny's."* I wanted to have the option to call her or run away to her house when life got hard. I looked for her throughout life; I looked for that love, her affection, that feeling, or that smell. I wanted to do her hair when she got too old to care. I wanted to pick up her groceries and put the food away.

These wants and desires would never come, nor would I ever have that special love again. I felt robbed throughout my life. With the brutal life I had ahead of me, I could've used her special love. It would've helped me through the obstacles I had to face. It was a significant loss for everyone. At only two years old, this was the beginning of my relationship with death. Yes, I had a relationship with death and an affair with life.

By this time, I was four years old. I started calling my Aunt Shelby "Mommy," and I called my mother "Aunt Queen." I knew she was my mother and not my aunt; all the other kids called her Aunt Queen, so I followed. We all lived together on Baltimore street with my grandfather. My grandfather was something else. We called him Granddaddy, and he didn't play. My cousins often said I was his favorite, but I didn't think so. I was just so afraid of a butt-whooping; I listened to whatever he said. The crazy part is we all hyped up the "butt whopping myth," and he rarely ever beat us. We were all his favorites.

Granddaddy was lazy around the house. He made us clean the bathtub after he got out and do whatever else he didn't enjoy doing. My cousin Darin would hate to clean out the bathtub. Granddaddy loved to soak in the bathtub and would always leave a massive ring around the tub when he got out. Darin would run whenever granddaddy called him; he would eventually get caught. It was always so funny to see him run from Granddaddy.

Diamond was sneaky and quiet. The quiet ones always get you in trouble; they act so innocent, especially in front of adults. Diamond was two years older than me. We grew up like sisters instead of cousins, and we shared the same interests. I was the weakest of the three of us. I was sensitive, and everything hurt my feelings. I'm sure this extreme sensitivity annoyed the hell out of my cousins.

It was an early Sunday morning, and I was sitting at the kitchen table watching Granddaddy make his famous sweet potato pie. We sang the Temptations song "My Girl." The song played on his old record player. I would find myself in a daze watching the record spin around and around. It was a mystery to my four-year-old mind. I wondered, *how could a spinning record create sound? Were there men inside the record player singing?* I snapped out of my daze and watched as Granddaddy whipped the sweet potatoes with the mixer. We continued to sing and laugh.

With no warning, he fell asleep, which he often did at the drop of a dime. Sweet potatoes were flying everywhere! They flew all over the table, all over the floor, and all over me. It was a massive mess. I knew for sure I would be in trouble, although it wasn't my fault. I let him sleep while I kept singing, laughing, and swinging my feet.

"Sunni!" Granddaddy yelled as he woke up with a bit of saliva dripping from the side of his mouth.

"Yes," I fearfully answered. My heart was beating fast as if it was about to come out of my chest.

"Girl, you let me go to sleep?" he asked in an aggressive, manly tone.

I didn't respond. I looked at Granddaddy with anticipation. He then took his big finger, wiped a big chunk of sweet potato pie off my cheek, and licked it.

"Damn, this would've been a good batch of pie," he said while smiling and licking the pie off the spoon.

"It sure would've, Granddaddy," I said while rubbing my finger in the pie bowl to get another taste.

We laughed and laughed. Little did I know at the time; this was considered a memory. I didn't understand these moments were precious, and they came far and few in between. That memory was dear to me and the beginning of my understanding of how to cherish these little happy moments in life as they wouldn't always be there.

We eventually moved out of Granddaddy's house, and he moved into a senior citizen building. We could visit him, but we couldn't live there. My mother worked on getting us a place of our own. We were on the waiting list for public housing. While we were waiting, we moved in with her godmother Sheila, her husband Big Kevin, and their three children.

Sheila had a daughter named Kesha, who smelled like a walking STD all the time. I can still remember the fish, urine, and old sperm smell she had whenever she walked by my little nose. They also had a son named Little Kevin; he was named after his father, Big Kevin. Little Kevin was labeled as an autistic child. He was kind, and although he was older, he made me feel like he was my age. Sheila's oldest child's name was Trayvon, and he was about 19. He stayed in the house a lot, not like most 19-year-old guys.

I was four years old and very talkative. Talking was my thing. I had a million and one questions.

"Mommy, why are we moving in with this lady?" I asked casually.

"Sunni, we are just staying here until our place comes through," she answered in a nonchalant tone.

"Why do Kesha smell like the fish Granddaddy cooks?" I asked with my nose frowned up.

She laughed, "I don't know Sunni. We won't be here for long, baby."

"Why did we have to move here anyway? I don't like these people," I said as I walked to get more of my clothes to put in a storage bin.

"Be quiet before someone hear you!" She put her index finger over her lips, and her body language showed she was agitated.

After multiple bold embarrassing questions, my mother finally told me to shut up. My mother worked nights at the video store. My mother and I would sleep on the sofa together, which had an annoying plastic cover. I despised sleeping on that damn sofa. I'd always wake up sweating or on the floor from sliding off the plastic cover. I never understood why people would try to reserve a sofa instead of enjoying the fabric it was made of. My mother always wanted me close to her. She would rather share a plastic sofa with me than have me sleep out of her sight.

Some nights when my mother was at work, Sheila would suggest I sleep in Kesha's room. Kesha peed on herself, and her room had a nasty smell just like her. The sheets were full of lint and carried a strong odor. The poor sheets had missed several laundry loads. I went into her room on super-hot days and laid in her stinky bed and watched her little fuzzy TV while she constantly told me to shut up. Kesha didn't enjoy talking at all. I'm sure everyone would classify my talking as annoying. As I must admit, I talked entirely too much. As much as I enjoyed talking, there was no pleasure in talking to her. She was unresponsive and nonchalant. During this period of my life, I missed my cousins, grandfather, and especially my Aunt Shelby.

As the months went on, I became close to Sheila's middle child Little Kevin. My talking didn't annoy him. Although he was an autistic child, he was brilliant, and he showed me how to do a lot of things around the house. He showed me how to pull the chair up to the refrigerator to sneak into the cabinet to get snacks. He knew right from wrong, and he was much more intelligent than everyone gave him credit for. He was overprotective, and he always wanted me to be with him.

By this time, Sheila's oldest child Trayvon initiated a relationship with me as well. He would bring me chips and juice from the corner store. When I'd come home from school, he would have gummy worms waiting for me on the living room table. Trayvon and Little Kevin didn't talk to each other much. Little Kevin acted weird when Trayvon was around. I thought maybe their relationship was distant because Trayvon wasn't Big Kevin's biological son. I became close with everyone in the house; I even grew on Kesha. I enjoyed living at Shelia's as the days went on.

The highlight of my day would be walking in the door and seeing my mother's beautiful face. Our schedules sometimes caused us to miss each other. When she came in, I would be asleep. No matter how much of a deep sleep I was in, I would smile whenever she lay on the plastic sofa. I could feel her presence, and I knew my mother was near. I really loved my mother. I loved her scent, her smile, and the way she hugged me. Our bond was strong, almost like we had special powers that connected us. Even at four years old I could look into my mother's eyes and tell if something was wrong.

Trayvon bought me more and more candy, and he spent more and more time with me. I enjoyed going to his room because he blasted the music super loud. He would act silly, dance, and pretend to be a rapper. He let me sing and dance too. He even let me jump on his bed. He would chase me around the house and tickle me. He would tickle me so severely that it would start to hurt. He would stop right before I began to cry. A little tickle made me laugh; more than a little made me uncomfortable. How could a tickle make you laugh with joy and cry with pain?

I became accustomed to being around everyone, and I was comfortable living there. I learned when to leave Kesha alone if she had an attitude and when it was ok to bother her. Little Kevin was my best friend, and Trayvon let me act like a big girl. I hardly ever talked to Sheila, but I truly enjoyed being around her husband, Big Kevin. He was fun and silly; he always made me laugh. Big Kevin seemed to enjoy life. He made the house more enjoyable.

One early afternoon I came home from school. The house was quiet and felt empty. I walked in and dropped my Minnie Mouse book bag by the front door. I saw a pack of candy worms, but it was empty. My eyes lit up for an empty bag of candy. It instantly annoyed me.

I called for my mother, "Ma!" she didn't answer.

"They all left for the market! What's wrong?" Trayvon screamed down the steps.

"Where are the gummy worms? Why is the pack empty?" I hollered up the steps.

"Come get them," he yelled back.

I sucked my teeth and walked up the steps. It seemed like it took forever to get to the top. I don't know if I was tired or just eager for the candy, but it seemed to be the longest walk ever. I entered his bedroom without knocking. The music was up loud, so he wouldn't have heard me knock anyway.

"Have you ever played the game Knick Knack Paddy Whack give a dog a bone?" he asked.

"No. Where is the candy?" I asked in an annoyed tone.

"This will be our new game. I'll give you the candy worms after we play," he smiled.

"Why do I have to wait? How do we play?" I questioned.

"The game goes like this, you hide, if I find you, I will chase you, and if I catch you, then you have to lick the dog's bone," he explained.

"Ok, I'll play," I agreed. It confused me, but all I heard was hide, run, fun, and candy worms after. So, I hid, he found me, he chased me, and he did, in fact, catch me. He softly grabbed my hand.

"Now we will go back to the room and do the last part of the game since I caught you," he advised.

He had on a stonewashed jumper with straps. He only had one side of the jumper strapped, and the other strap hung recklessly. He removed the metal hook from the one attached strap, and his jumper dropped. He was now standing there in his white t-shirt, boxer briefs, and long white socks.

"Now you must lick the bone," he reasoned. He pulled his penis from the hole in his boxer briefs and held it in his hand.

"Where is the bone?" I ignorantly asked.

"Right here," he answered. His free hand pointed to his penis.

"Where do I lick?" I asked as I moved closer to see.

"Right here," he said as he directed me to lick the head of his penis.

I felt funny, but I didn't know why. I licked as Trayvon instructed. His penis was already hard, but I had never seen a big penis before. I remembered taking baths with my cousin Darin, Aunt Shelby's son, but we were young kids, and his penis didn't look like Trayvon's bone. I didn't relate a naked man as being a threat. In my 4-year-old mind, we all have bodies; it was just skin. I had no fear of Trayvon or his bone. My innocent little mind couldn't comprehend how wrong it was to lick his bone.

In my mind, it was part of the game, right? Little did I know the bone was his nasty man piece, and I would lose my innocence on this day, playing this dumb ass game. He often made statements like, "Don't stop, and I'll buy you more candy tomorrow." I licked his bone until I wanted to stop, or he told me to stop. Sometimes I looked up at him and noticed his eyes were closed. That always confused me.

I remember thinking to myself that *if I can lick the bone, maybe I should bite the bone too.* He would constantly remind me that this was "OUR little game." We made this game up, so no need to tell anyone about it. One day, I remember telling my mother that we played Knick Knack Paddy Whack. She didn't know the details of the game, or she would have killed him without a second thought.

I didn't keep anything from my mother. She was my best friend. My mother always told me not to let anyone touch my private area, and she always made sure she bathed me. My mother also told me not to trust men or strangers. She was overprotective. Although she told me these things, he didn't do those things to me. He never touched my private area or physically penetrated me, nor did he ever give me a bath. So how would I know to inform my mother of this evil child molesting game? Licking his bone caused me no physical harm, so I couldn't comprehend how wrong it was. He was smart and manipulative, as most predators are. We all know the DEVIL can slither in any little crack, and he found one.

We played this game about three times whenever no one was home. One afternoon Little Kevin came home early while Knick Knack Paddy Whack was going on. As usual, Trayvon had the music blasting, so he didn't hear Little Kevin walk into his bedroom. I saw Little Kevin's eyes get big. He looked at me with a look I had never seen on his face before, almost like a look of disappointment. He then looked up at Trayvon with anger. His eyebrows were raised.

"NO SUNNI, GET UP!" he screamed. He pulled me up by my arm with force and shook me.

"Ok, Ok," I cried as I slowly stood up.

"Don't you ever do that again. EVER! Don't come into this room again or talk to Trayvon again. Do you hear me?" Little Kevin screamed.

"Yes, I heard you! Let go of my arm," I cried.

"Don't tell anyone about this. It will only make the adults mad," he demanded in a firm voice.

"Tell anyone what? That me and Trayvon were playing a game?" I questioned.

"It's not a game! Don't play anything with him and stay away from him," he screamed with agitation in his voice.

He said it right in front of Trayvon, and Trayvon said nothing. Not one word. I felt confused, and I wanted to run away from this tense situation. I was angry with Little Kevin for grabbing me with so much aggression. I thought to myself, *did I do something wrong? Why is Little Kevin so upset? Why did Trayvon rush and pull up his pants to hide his bone?*

I trusted Little Kevin, so I told no one. I thought it would be stupid to tell someone about a dumb game and how Little Kevin flipped out. Ignorance is the root of most pain. *Should I have known a penis was not a bone in a game? Should a four-year-old know what a penis looks like? Should I have explained the game to my mother so that she could have blown his fucking head off? Should I have questioned Trayvon saying this was OUR little game?* This was too much thinking for a four-year-old.

What I did know is I would stay away from Trayvon, as Little Kevin said. After that day, Trayvon avoided me. Little Kevin seemed to hate him. The house developed a weird vibe. I stayed under my mother, where I didn't have to overthink. We moved out shortly after. Our place finally came through. At first, my mother would still talk to Sheila on the phone here and there, but months would go by, then years. I didn't tell my mother about the disgusting act Trayvon made me perform, nor did I fully understand it at the time. My biggest regret was not taking a bite off that BITCH'S BONE!

CHAPTER 3

IN MY PROJECTS

We left Sheila's house and moved into our own place. We moved into Perkins Projects in East Baltimore. I was so excited to be moving into a house with just my mother and me. This was our first place of our own. I wasn't aware of what the projects were. All I understood was we moved out of Sheila's into our own house. I had no clue or interest in what kind of environment we were moving in. I got to be in my own room, and that's what mattered to me. I prayed I would never have to sleep on Shelia's plastic sofa ever again. I never forgot how it damn near suffocated me every night.

The day we moved into Perkins Projects, Aunt Shelby, Granddaddy, and Uncle Lee talked and fried fish in the kitchen. Uncle Lee was Aunt Shelby's husband and Granddaddy's best friend. Uncle Lee was funny, silly, and a joy to be around. He and Granddaddy would go fishing every week. There is nothing like fresh fish. My favorite fish was Spots. Granddaddy taught all his kids how to clean and cook fish. His fried fish was always the best. I listened as they all sat around the kitchen talking. Granddaddy was in preaching mode.

"Queen, don't get stuck in this environment. Use this place as a stepping stone, and don't get caught up," Granddaddy said as he looked directly into her eyes.

"I know, Daddy. This place is temporary."

"I'm just telling you, don't let this place change you, child! Don't become where you live," he said in an antagonizing way.

"Daddy, I know, don't worry. I'll only be here two years tops, and then we're gone," she quickly responded as if she wanted to end the conversation.

"Sunni go on the front steps while we talk," Aunt Shelby said as she noticed I was listening.

I made a guilty face as if they caught me doing something wrong. I knew kids weren't allowed in grown folks' conversations. I'd always listen as much as I could before getting caught. I took a moment to think about what I heard. I really took in what Granddaddy told my mother. At the time, I didn't understand how profound those words were. It felt like he was preaching, but it stuck with me for some reason. Those words would one day have a substantial impact on our lives. My grandfather had wisdom, and he didn't talk nonsense.

I left the kitchen and ran down the steps toward the front door. I went to the front door in amazement. I remember thinking, *what is this place? It looks so fun*. There were so many kids playing and chasing each other. Kids were screaming and yelling while riding their bikes and scooters. I looked over to the side of me, and I saw my neighbor sitting on the steps drinking a beer. I heard people yelling through the courts (courts are split areas in the projects with different names), "A Yoooo." I heard the song "You Can't Touch This" by MC Hammer blasting from the cars riding by.

There was a woman in the window with pillows under her arms as if she had been there so long that she had to get comfortable. There was so much chaos, and I loved it. It was exciting to see all these people outside. This was my first time visiting the projects, let alone living there. After some time, my mom called me to unpack. I ran into my new room and unpacked. I was excited to put everything exactly where I wanted it.

As nightfall came, there were still people talking, laughing, and screaming outside. They were so loud, and it felt like they were in the bedroom with me. I was not too fond of the nighttime noise. It was overwhelming. I was an only child, and I liked it to be quiet at night, so I could read a book or pray to God. I loved God for as long as I could remember. We always had a special relationship. I loved reading just as much. Little did I know, those peaceful quiet nights of praying and reading were OVER! People in the projects don't sleep.

There are many categories of people in the projects. Let me explain. There are the straight-up bums that do absolutely nothing all day but take up the air God gives us. They don't clean, they don't cook, and they barely wash their asses. They wake up around 1:00 p.m. every day, and they're always late. Surprisingly, they feel like someone owes them something, although they do absolutely nothing.

Some people felt they were better than everyone else, but they didn't want to pay regular rent prices, so they stayed in low-income housing instead. They walked around with snobby attitudes and always bragged about what nice area they came from. They never let you forget that they can afford to live somewhere else. They don't let their kids play with the other project kids, and they usually dress them up and leave the projects daily. They typically have jobs, but they steal from the system and get food stamps and other government assistance, just like everyone else.

There are the baby makers, and these fast women usually grew up in the projects. They have multiple kids by different men in every court. They had low self-esteem, no confidence, and no respect for their bodies. They just yearned for attention, and if took 15 different dicks to get it, then that's what they did. They lacked morals. Most of them didn't have a father, so any man they met became their daddy. We also had the freak ball sluts who had sex with any and everything moving. I referred to them as the walking STDs of the projects.

I wouldn't dare forget about the window watchers. They sit in their windows with their pillows all day long, just to be nosey and tell everyone's business. They eat food in the window. They talk on their cordless phone in the window. They smoke cigarettes in the window, and I've even seen them sleep in the window. Their entire purpose in life is to gossip and be in other people's business. They know everything and everyone. They are often too afraid to leave the window out of fear of missing some drama.

Oh, let's talk about the mighty beggars—the ones who always need something, whether it's a quarter or the drawers off your ass. No matter how much you give them, they will surely beg again the next time they see you, now, this could even be ten minutes later. There are no time limits for begging in the projects. There are no rules for begging. They could ask for a quarter, sugar, butter, socks, a puff off your cigarette, a sip of your soda, or a few dollars towards their next high.

There were intelligent people in the projects. They loved school. They didn't belong in the projects. They were forced to be there because of poverty, not by choice. They'd always get skipped two grades ahead because they really belonged in a better school. A school where they could excel, but the school system goes by your zip code, so it didn't matter if they were brilliant; they still got stuck with the rest of us.

Now onto the projects' badass chicks, they wore all designer clothes, kept their hair done, and spent all their government money on materialistic things. They dressed up every day, just to walk around the projects. Their government check would be gone by the second week of the month. Their reckless spending habits would cause them to borrow soap and dish detergent all month.

Oh, the filthy dirty people. Soap was not their friend, but roaches were. They ran from toothpaste and deodorant. Their houses were disgusting and scary, to say the least. Let's not forget about the ugly people who were usually shit starters because they were unattractive, which made them mad at the world. The unattractive people walked around the projects fighting all day. Their goal was to make you unattractive like them.

I can't forget about all the beautiful people in the projects, the ones who just stayed there to make it a better place and to provide more opportunities for the less fortunate. They fight for the cause, and they attend city meetings to try to make the projects a better environment. They volunteer at the schools to make a difference. They try to help the kids who are falling behind, and they fight against violence.

Lastly and most importantly is the flow of the economy in the projects. We had a money system. The drug dealers provide the drugs, weed, coke, crack, or dope. The consumer was the addict, and that person usually used the government's money to pay for their habit. People cooked and sold dinners to make money, also using (government food stamps). The kitchen beauticians were women who did hair better than most hair salons, and they got paid for their talents.

Money coming in is money going out, but it always stayed in the project community. The drug dealers' profit was spent back into the projects by buying a plate of food, paying to get his girlfriend's hair done, giving little kids dollars all day, letting the addicts purchase drugs when they were short on cash, and paying people's rent to avoid an eviction. The cash system worked. So, where did I fit in these categories of people? Absolutely nowhere! Yet.

My first project love was a girl. I was only seven years old when I first laid eyes on her. I thought to myself; she *is BEAUTIFUL!* She was 15 years old. I instantly admired the way she walked, talked, and carried herself. I thought, *who is she?* She had beautiful caramel skin, with big full lips, and her eyes were slanted like an almond. She favored Toni Braxton. As I daydreamed about who she was in my mind, in a blink of an eye, I looked up, and she had disappeared. I didn't see her again for a few days. Then out of nowhere, there she was, walking towards me. I smiled.

"Hi, does Queen live here?" she questioned. She looked around as if she wasn't sure she had the right house.

"Yes, that's my mother," I proudly said.

"Oh, I'm Honey. Do you think she can do my hair?"

"Yes, she's upstairs. I don't think she has any clients today. You can come in with me," I insisted.

I thought to myself, *girl, your hair looks fine, and what kind of name is Honey?* I walked her upstairs to get my mother. I wasn't sexually attracted to her, but I instantly admired her. She started getting her hair done every week, and I would talk her head off every week. She would often call me crazy. We talked about everything. I mean EVERYTHING! She became my big sister. I looked up to her. Honey spent all her extra time with me.

Honey had two brothers but no sisters. The fact I looked up to her was flattering to her. I became her best friend. Little did I know; many people didn't like her. Maybe they were just jealous. She was funny, and she had so much personality. I couldn't understand why everyone wouldn't want to be around her. The love she gave me would last a lifetime, and we built an unbreakable bond. My first project love was my big sister Honey.

The projects will break you sooner or later. No one is immune to the bullshit. A few years went by, and I was sitting on the front steps eating a freeze pop and enjoying the summer heat. I lived in Dallas Court. By this time, I knew everyone in my court. I also knew a few kids from other courts. Some kids were mean, and some kids were only friendly when they had no one else to play with. Mrs. Macy was my neighbor who watched me while my mother went to work. I liked Mrs. Macy. She sold cookies, candy, chips, and frozen cups out of her house. I got off the front steps to play with Ms. Macy's granddaughter, Fats.

Fats lived in Spring Court, but she often came to her grandmother's house, so we played a lot. On this day, some other girls were around instigating, and Fats kept being mean and rude towards me.

"Fats, you should just smack her!" one girl suggested.

"Why would she do that? We are friends," I asked.

"Why would she do that? We are friends. Blah blah blah," another girl marked me.

"You know what, I don't like you anymore, come on, let's fight," Fats said. She stood up to get in a fighting position.

"What? You going to show off for these girls?" I asked with a confused look.

She pulled my arm, "Get up, let's fight!"

I thought, *is she serious? She wants to show off for these girls and fight me? Her friend?* After she pulled again, I got up, but I wasn't mentally prepared to fight my friend. It was stupid, and it hurt my feelings. She hit me, and we fought. I fought back, but I didn't try to hurt her. In my mind, she was still my friend. There was blood in my hair from the back of my head hitting the concrete. This was my first hood lesson; a weak heart will get you killed in these projects. At only eight years old, I learned one of the most valuable lessons in life. <u>Don't trust females. Make them earn your trust!</u> My mother came home from work and fussed me out when she learned I was in a fight and I didn't protect myself. As she washed the blood out of my hair, she started asking questions about the fight.

"Why didn't you protect yourself? Why did you let her make you bleed? What happened?" she questioned.

"Ma, she was my friend. I don't know why I let her get the best of me," I cried.

"Fuck her! I'm your only friend around here. Remember that Sunni," she yelled.

That was harsh advice that I indeed needed to survive in this new environment. I had no answers as to why I let Fats control the fight. I felt betrayed and weak. I stayed in the house for two days out of shame and embarrassment. I was such a sensitive and kind-hearted kid at this age. My heart was pure and warm. I didn't know how to become cold, even if I was surrounded by ice. I was genuinely a good person. A few days later, Fats wanted to play as if nothing happened. She said sorry, and I forgave her. This became the unhealthy cycle of our friendship.

When the girls came around again, my heart thumped with anxiety. I was afraid, not because I had to fight again, but because I knew this time I had to defend myself. As expected, Fats called me mean names and started saying she only played with me because her grandmother made her. The feeling of betrayal was less intense this time. I expected nothing less from a coward.

"Do you want to fight again because they are here?" I asked.

She didn't speak. I stood up and looked at her with fearless eyes.

"Do you want to fight?" I asked again.

"No thanks, I beat you up already," she boldly said while hunching her shoulders.

"I let you beat me up but try it again now," I spoke sternly.

They all laughed. They made statements like, "Who lets someone beat them up?"

I felt overwhelmed as the laughter got more and more under my skin. I repeated myself, and Fats just laughed. As she laughed, I punched her in the nose and kept swinging until my arms couldn't physically move. The adrenaline was so intense. I couldn't even feel her punches toward me. I must honestly say, I felt so good after the fight. It felt good to protect myself. I thought for the first time since we moved, *maybe I'm getting the hang of this project thing.*

We reconciled a week later and remained friends. I always cared for her, but I always knew not to trust her. She switched up whenever certain people came around. I decided not to take it personally when she changed. I realized she wasn't strong. Following other people was her way of fitting in. We were kids, so we let go of the pettiness fast. In the projects, you fight and make up overnight. You will eventually be with the same people because it's a small community. You have no choice but to deal with them again at some point. When you are only eight years old, you don't care enough to hold a grudge. I learned early in life how to deal with people accordingly. I also learned fear is not always a negative thing, because a scared person could hurt you. I embraced my fear. I told myself *I would fight as much as necessary to protect myself.*

Little did I know, that would be a lot of fighting. Girls in the projects wanted to fight for everything! They wanted to fight because I was light-skinned, because I was skinny, because I had hair, because I didn't say hi, because I played with someone else, because a boy liked me, or for absolutely no reason at all. I realized poor people are fucking angry! At that moment, I made my mind up not to be poor and not to be angry. I had no interest in turning 18 years old to apply for public housing.

Was I poor too at the time? Yes, I was! I had no more or no less. In my mind, I was full of riches. I never thought I was better than anyone, but I always wanted better. When you live in the projects, we are family; we are equal. No matter what more you think you have, we are all equal. Even when you move out of the projects, you are still family. The project community creates a bond for life. No one is ever better. I understood that well; however, I always wanted more. I wasn't ashamed to voice that I wanted a better life. For that reason, many people didn't like me, and eventually, I learned not to give a fuck!

CHAPTER 4

GUT INSTINCT

Sweets was my best friend. She didn't live in the projects, but she came to her Aunt Niecy's house almost every day. We became best friends because people said we favored each other. She called me her twin. The name "Twin" stuck. Other people called us twins too. Sweets was beautiful, so it was a compliment in my eyes. She had caramel skin with big full lips and a cute little nose. She was just a little slimmer and a little darker than me.

It was a hot summer day in the middle of July. School had just let out a few weeks prior. Sweets and I loved when school let out because she wouldn't have to go back home every night. She could spend the night with me, or I could spend the night with her at her Aunt Niecy's house. I loved her Aunt Niecy like she was my aunt. Aunt Niecy showed no favoritism between us. She would curse all of us out, including her two daughters. Aunt Niecy put us out of her house on a regular basis. Sometimes I would walk right into a curse-out. I would think, *damn, what did I do? I just walked in here*. It was all love, so I didn't get offended.

Sweets and I were walking from the corner store after getting some penny candy. I loved penny candy, especially the strawberry ones. The sun was blazing on our skin as we walked; it felt like a hundred degrees. As we walked from the store, Sweets suddenly stopped.

"It's hot!" she blurted out.

"Are you ok? Why did you stop walking like that?" I curiously asked.

"Yes, Mommy, I'm ok!" she responded in a sarcastic voice.

"You know you be scaring me, girl!"

"I'm about to walk back to the store for an ice cream," she said. She completely disregarded my comment.

"It's hot as hell, but I don't feel like walking back. Just meet me in Spring Court at the playground," I said as I fanned my face with my hand and lightly wiped the sweat off my forehead.

"Noooo, come on, Twin, walk back with me," she whined.

"Nope, don't feel like it," I said in a stern voice.

Sweets rolled her eyes, called me lazy, and walked back toward the store. I walked the opposite way. I was walking and singing SWV's song "Weak." I often sang out loud, as if I could actually sing. I was hitting a high note when a boy named Toni rode by on his bike. Toni was about 15 years old and known for always playing too much and smiling for no reason. Toni had deep dimples, and he loved to show them off with his big pearly white teeth.

"Kick out your candy!" he yelled. He pointed his hand like a gun with his index finger pointing toward me.

"So Toni, your petty ass is robbing little girls for candy now?" I laughed.

"Kick it out girl," he smiled.

"Here, boy, you are only worth five cents," I tossed him five pieces of penny candy.

"You're only worth one cent," he chuckled. He then threw a piece of candy back at me.

I smiled and put up my middle finger.

"Now that's not ladylike, especially coming from a young lady who CAN'T sing."

I laughed and hunched my shoulders because I knew he caught me singing.

"Next time I'm a stick you up for all your candy!" he barked. Toni rode off, popping a wheelie on his bike.

I gave him the middle finger again and crossed the street. I cut through Mason Court and ran into my sister Honey. Her hair was in a dark black bang and a long ponytail, with Chinese chopsticks on each side. She was wearing a short form-fitting denim dress, but not too short like a club outfit. Honey had nice legs and hips, so she could pull off wearing any dress.

"Honey, where are you going?" I yelled to catch her attention.

"Hey, baby!" she said with excitement. She told the guy she was with to wait for a minute.

"UMMM, what are you up to?" I asked with a suspicious facial expression.

"I'll give you all the scoop later about this Cat," she said, referring to the tall, dark guy she was with at the time.

"You know I'll be waiting up to hear all the details," I smiled and rubbed my hands together in anticipation of the juicy tea, she was sure to spill.

"Girl, you are a mess. Here are five dollars for you to go to the store or something. Let me go. We'll talk later."

She walked back to the guy's black-tinted-out Honda, and they pulled off. Although Honey was much older than me, I was literally her best friend. She told me everything. I loved to imagine I was in her world. I would imagine her stories and quietly listen for every detail. Some of the guys she talked about, I would picture they were in love with me. My imagination could go far beyond my usual thoughts. There were no secrets between us. I thought about going back to the store and getting a snowball since Honey had just given me five dollars. For some strange reason, my gut instincts said don't go back to the store.

Just as the thought crossed my mind, I heard massive gunshots. It sounded like fireworks on the fourth of July. I ran towards the playground and immediately thought about Sweets and got worried. I had this bad feeling in the pit of my stomach. I naturally worried about Sweets anyway; I feared for her like an overprotective mother. Sweets was ill. She was always sick because of health issues. The doctors didn't expect her to live past the age of 12, so I always had a fear of losing her. I cherished every moment with her, even when she got on my nerves. I'd always think in the back of my mind I could lose her any day, so let me be nice.

I think she knew my weakness for her, and she used it to her advantage any chance she got. I didn't care because I loved her. I was naturally a sensitive creature and full of emotions. My heart allowed me to feel everything. Suddenly, I thought about Honey. She and that guy just pulled off in his car. The gunshots happened so rapidly; I thought, *could Honey and the guy be hurt?* Now my mind was racing even more, and my thoughts were all over the place. To calm my mind, I decided that Honey was ok; she had to be! I'm now back concerned about Sweets since she was in the direction of the gunshots. As I was running from the gunfire, something just didn't feel right. I started to panic more, so I stopped running and stood on the side of someone's steps.

"Hey, you can come in here!" a woman yelled from her window.

"I can't. I have to find my friend Sweets. I left her at the store, and the gunshots are coming from that way!" I yelled back.

"Hunni, sometimes you have to worry about yourself, just run over!"

In that moment of panic, I thought, *what the hell does she mean to just worry about myself? Did she not hear me say I left Sweets at the store?* I didn't understand the thought process of selfishness. I knew she meant well by trying to help me to safety, but It didn't matter. I was already annoyed. There were too many thoughts rambling through my mind, and some nosey woman in the window was not one.

I was out of breath and sweating profusely. The heat was draining me. I prayed aloud, "God, please protect Sweets, God, please let her be ok, God please, God, please." The gunshots finally stopped, or maybe they had been stopped, but I didn't notice because of all the distractions. I took in three deep breaths and began to walk back towards the corner store. I heard people screaming, "Nooooo Noooooo Noooooo!"

I began to walk slower out of fear I would see the crowd standing over Sweets. The noise became overwhelming. The chaos was just too much for my mind to process. My feet stopped moving, and I became paralyzed. My thoughts started to take over my physical body. I told myself, *keep walking, don't let fear stop you*. I kept thinking *I should've walked back to the store with her. Why did I leave her?*

I convinced myself to walk a few more steps; my feet were heavy. I saw the crowd hovering in a circle. I looked over and saw a bike in the street. The bike looked lonely; it was out of place. It was so far from the crowd. It didn't belong. I continued to get closer to the crowd, and the screaming became louder. I saw "The Shoe." That Fila shoe instantly made my heart drop. I got closer, and I saw it was Toni's body in a puddle of blood. He was limp, and his brains were scattered all over the ground. His bone particles, skin debris, and a massive amount of blood covered the brick wall. He was unrecognizable.

I heard someone yell, "Sunni!" I turned around with tears and sorrow in my eyes. It was Sweets. I felt a sense of relief, and we hugged and cried for what felt like five minutes. We didn't speak, we just cried. My heart was heavy. I replayed in my mind the conversation Toni and I had only minutes prior to his death. I pictured his smile and remembered how he rode away on his bike so happy. I thought, *how could he be gone that fast? We were just laughing a few minutes ago.* I thought of his mother, who simply adored him. I started to cry more.

I couldn't bring myself to look at his corpse again, so I kept looking at the Fila shoe. Sweets grabbed my hand and said, "Let's go, Twin." I was a young child seeing a dead body for the first time. I had nightmares for weeks. I prayed to God for the images to leave me. I couldn't even look at Fila's shoes anymore without thinking about that day. I thought of Toni daily and replayed our last conversation repeatedly. I prayed he didn't see it coming, and he died a swift, painless death. He was truly a sweet young guy. I later found out they murdered Toni for $15 petty dollars. His death changed my life forever. Unfortunately, this was just another day in the projects.

CHAPTER 5

TOO YOUNG AND INNOCENT FOR THAT BOX!

I went with my mother to an unfamiliar house on Biddle Street on the weekends. Biddle Street was for sure the hood, but it wasn't my hood. The city became foreign to me, I'd much rather be at home running around in the courts. My mother went there to smoke weed with the "fat sisters." That's what I called them as a kid.

Their names were Kat and Robby. I didn't know where these heavier friends came from. Kat was shaped weirdly; she had a big back and a small lower half. Robby was just heavy. Now I loved my big women and never cared about anyone's size, shape, or looks. It still didn't stop me from wondering where my mother found this group of heavier friends. I never saw them at my house or with Aunt Shelby.

The sisters lived up the street from a Chinese joint that had the best shrimp egg rolls. When I thought about going to Biddle street, the food was what I looked forward to more than anything. Although I was slim, I loved to eat. The sisters always had food in abundance. Food was a pleasure of mine, and if it weren't for my fast metabolism, I would've been just as big as the sisters. I was forced to hang out with their niece Sandy. She was conceited and stuck so far up her own ass that it made no sense. I had no other options in this new hood, so I played with her. If I were back home, she would be an enemy.

I disliked kids that were "too cute for this and too cute for that." I liked to play, and I was never too cute to have fun. I often called her "Ms. Stuck Up." I couldn't understand why my mother was going all the way to the city to smoke weed with Robby and Kat when there was plenty of weed down the projects. Kat was a nasty thang. She had pictures of dicks all over her wall. Big poster-sized photos of naked strippers hanging over the bed. Handcuffs on each side of her headboard, with exotic magazines all over the floor.

The adults made me sit in Kat's room while they smoked weed. I don't know whose brilliant idea that was. The first time I went into her room, I was amazed. I looked through all her nasty stuff and giggled. On one particular day, I made the mistake of touching her overly-used vibrator and ran to the bathroom to wash my hands. Robby was cute in the face and much friendlier than Kat. She treated me like she treated her niece. Their other sister Max was nice as well. Max was the mother of the stuck-up niece Sandy. Max was a church-going woman and lived on a more relaxed side of town.

There I was, sitting on the steps, when this thick, light brown-skinned guy, with noticeably brown eyes, walked over.

"You must be Queen's daughter," he inquired. He looked at me with excitement.

"That would be me, the one and only," I responded with a smile.

"I'm Smoke. Nice to meet you," he chuckled.

"Nice to meet you as well, Smoke."

I looked at him and shook his big hand. He then opened the door and went into the Sister's house. I'd seen him before, but I didn't pay him any mind. That night we left late, around 3 a.m. Smoke walked us to a cab. On the ride home, my mother started asking questions.

"What do you think about Smoke?" she nervously asked.

"Nothing," I mumbled.

"Well, you know I tell you everything, right?"

I nodded my head with heavy drifting eyes, "Yes, Mommy, I know."

"I'm kind of dating him," she smirked and waited for my response.

"Oh, that's why we keep coming up here? I thought you didn't like the weed down Perkins."

She laughed, "No girl, Kat, and Robby are Smoke's sisters. I'm just dating their brother, but the weed at home is just fine."

Everything was making sense now. We came to the fat house for the fat brother. Smoke bought my mother everything. He purchased her gold bracelets, necklaces, clothes, and fancy coats. Every time she came around, he had a new gift for her. The sisters told my mother their brother was no good. Smoke wasn't my mother's type, so she figured she could use him since he wasn't any good anyway. The problem with her plan was that Smoke grew on her, and she eventually fell in love with him.

He moved in with us and later proposed. I always wanted my mother to be happy, but I never cared for him. He was friendly, but there was just a bad vibe that he gave me. He was a bad influence on my mother. As time went by, he eventually convinced my mother to try a coolie. A coolie is a cigarette with cocaine and tobacco mixed. Back in the early 90s, it was no big deal to smoke a coolie. Some people mixed weed with cocaine. It was a casual high until it became not so casual. My mother would only smoke coolies as a fun high. Just when she went to Biddle street with the sisters or when she was hanging with Smoke. I'm not blaming anyone for the start of my mother smoking coolies, but birds of a feather flock together.

Smoke had two kids, Jazz, and Little Smoke. Jazz's mother was on heavy drugs, so Jazz often stayed with us at our house. Smoke truly loved Jazz. She looked just like him. I was an only child and not used to sharing anything. I didn't want to share my room, my mother, my time, or anything else. Jazz was four-years-old, so sweet and soft-spoken. She wanted my mother to be her mother, and I was jealous. I should've been more understanding of her needs, as she was only four years old and missed her own mother. I was so mean to her. She followed me everywhere, and my mother made me take Jazz everywhere.

"Sunni, take Jazz outside with you," my mother demanded.

"Ma, I'm going with my friends. It won't be any little kids," I responded in an annoyed, pleading tone.

"Just do what I said, or you can stay in here," my mother yelled.

"Ugh," I mumbled under my breath.

"Jazz go get your jacket and go outside, baby," she calmly told Jazz.

"Thanks, Mommy," Jazz replied with eagerness. With a big smile, she ran to get a jacket and hugged my mother.

The first time she called my Queen "Mommy," I almost snapped. "She is not your mother!" I screamed.

My mother got upset and called me to her bedroom for a talk. I slowly walked to her room because I dreaded getting in trouble. Instead of yelling, my mother just talked to me. We talked about how Jazz needed love and how she had been through a lot. My mother explained that no one could ever take my place or come between our bond, but Jazz was younger and needed our affection. I thought about how I would've felt if I was taken away from my mother and placed in a new environment. I softened my attitude and sympathized with Jazz. My mother always had a way of making me see things from a different perspective. After our talk, I instantly change my attitude.

Jazz was now my little four-year-old sister. I loved her, and I embraced her love. I protected her, and it became fun always having someone else around. I took her under my wing. When I went outside, my little sister was coming too. I did her hair, and we played dress-up. I shared everything with her. She was so thrilled to have a big sister.

One late night, I came downstairs to get something to drink, and Jazz was attempting to drink my asthma medicine, prednisone. I had to tell on her because I caught her trying to drink medicine before. My mother talked to Jazz about the dangers of drugs. My mother told Smoke about how Jazz tried to drink my medication, and he beat her. That was the side of Smoke I didn't like. Yes, he loved Jazz very much, and she adored him too; however, his anger would escalate very fast. That was the mean side of him that came creeping out now and then.

I felt so bad for snitching. What made me feel even worse was after Jazz got her butt spanked, she lay under me in the bed while weeping softly. I put my arm around her, and from that day forward, I grew a deep emotional bond with her. She needed me to protect her. Even after I told on her, she still felt safe to cuddle with me. I explained that I had to tell because drinking medicine is dangerous and could make her ill. She simply said, "It's ok sister, I still love you." We later found out Jazz had a thing for medicine. She craved it. We heard my mother and Smoke arguing about him beating her. After that day, my mother took extra precautions to hide all the medicine in the house.

Jazz would often hang outside with me, Sweets, and my other friend B. We would have to ditch Jazz if we wanted to be mischievous or misbehave, like kissing boys in the Tot Lot. The Tot Lot was our little place where we'd go to do whatever we didn't want the adults to see what we were doing. B was my best friend too, and Sweets didn't like it at all. B was a short, light-skinned girl with thick eyebrows. I always loved her full eyebrows; they were dark and seemed to have a mind of their own. B and I became close because she always stayed the same, unlike other phony girls in the projects.

B was my everyday best friend. Sweets would leave to go home most of the week, but B and I went to school together. I didn't compare the two, and I just wanted them to get along. I wanted them to see what I saw in both of them. Then maybe they could say, "Oh, that's why Sunni likes her." That never happened. They never got into a physical fight; they just didn't click. They didn't like each other. After a while, I stop trying and just kept them apart. I hung out with them separately.

Every so often, Jazz's mother would beg Smoke to give her back. She would lie and say she was clean. She always had a story of how she was no longer on drugs. Smoke knew how much Jazz loved her mother and would eventually give in and let her go back. I really missed her when she left. The house became quiet, and I would be the only child again. But I knew she would be back. She ALWAYS came back.

By this time, Smoke and my mother were married. Jazz and I were a part of the wedding, looking as cute as we could be. I was so happy to see her again. She had been staying with her mom for a few months. Jazz came back with us after the wedding. Smoke and my mother decided Jazz would live with us permanently since her mother was still messing up badly with drugs. That fast, I had my sister back. I was excited, and so was she. This time around, Jazz kept talking about her mother and how she missed her. She would even cry at night.

My mother and Smoke started fighting a lot. Smoke was cheating with a woman that he had on the side for years. He had this side chick before he even met my mother. She was one of those round-the-way girls that a man never leaves alone. Most hood guys have one. When my mother found out he was dealing with his side chick, she wanted to leave him.

My mother stayed because she cared so much for Jazz, and honestly, she wanted to fight for her marriage. Smoke cried and pleaded that he would never betray her again. They eventually worked through their issues and stayed together. Jazz's mother called and asked if Jazz could come home for the weekend. At first, Smoke told her no, she couldn't go. Jazz overheard him on the phone and instantly got excited.

"Is that my mother? Is she coming to get me?" Jazz asked with bright, bubbly eyes.

"Yes, Jazz, this is your mother, but do you remember what we talked about? Mommy needs time to get better," he softly said as he knew she would be disappointed.

"But I miss her," she cried.

"I know Jazz, but…" he was interrupted by Jazz's mother yelling on the phone.

"Daddy, please. Just for the weekend. I'll come right back, Daddy," she smiled innocently.

Smoke felt bad and let her go with her mother for the weekend. That was the worst mistake ever. Jazz's mother was on the methadone program; however, she was still using street drugs. The point of being on the program is to stop using hardcore street drugs and take methadone as a legal replacement drug. The first night Jazz got there with her mother; she drank some of her mother's methadone from the refrigerator. Jazz told her mother that she drank it, and her mother fussed at her and then sent her to bed. Methadone is a potent drug for adults and only to be used in small doses.

The next afternoon Jazz's mother went to wake her up. Jazz was an early bird and usually woke up at the crack of dawn. It was after lunchtime when her mother finally thought of her child not being up yet. She tried to wake her up, but Jazz wouldn't move. She was no longer breathing. She had lost her color, and her temperature was cold.

My precious, calm, sweet little sister was gone. She drank half of the bottle of methadone and died in her sleep. Her mother called Smoke and told him their daughter had died. Smoke went nuts, and began to cry hysterically. He punched a hole in the wall and just fell to the floor in agony. I came into the house from outside to get something to drink and saw Smoke and my mother crying on the floor.

"What's wrong?" I asked.

"Come here, baby. I don't know how to tell you this, but Jazz is gone," my mother softly cried.

"I know, but she'll be back. She always comes back."

Smoke yelled with pain in his voice, "Not this time, not this time, she is dead, my baby girl is dead!"

Before understanding how or why Jazz died, I just fell to the floor and cried with them. I thought again, *that fast, she was just here. She just left yesterday. How could she be gone?* I was devastated. I had to say goodbye to my little sister. I started to care for Smoke because his love for Jazz was so strong. He became very vulnerable around us. I made a little memorial on my desk in my room with all her things. I missed her like crazy. I cried a lot. I wanted to hear her say the word "sister" just one more time.

We went to her funeral. It was an early service. Jazz wore a pretty pink dress. I couldn't see her shoes in the coffin, but I hoped she had on the white patent leather ones with the little heel that she loved to clap around in the house. She looked so peaceful in the coffin. I remember looking down at her and admiring her pretty long eyelashes. They were stiff and curled. Her lips were dry and cracked. I wanted to give her some of my bubble gum lip gloss that she loved so much. Her face was partially smashed from laying on it in a sleep position for so long while being deceased. I touched her precious hand, and it was freezing cold. I immediately jumped back.

I looked at her again, and I thought to myself, *this is Jazz; she is gone*. I found the courage to touch her hand again, and it was still cold. I counted her fingers for some strange reason. At that very moment is when I realized I would never hear her voice again, nor would she ever use my lip gloss, call my name, or call my mother "mommy," or follow my every move or lay under me after she got in trouble. My heart became heavy. I thought to myself; *she is really gone*. I dreamed of her for weeks, maybe even months. Death was just lurking in the shadows, following me, haunting me, and waiting for me. Death was coming for my life.

After losing Jazz, everything changed. Smoke began to smoke straight cocaine in front of my mother. He told my mother to try it without the nicotine, and she would feel amazing after. The first time she declined. The next time he offered, she accepted. The high was like nothing she'd ever experienced before. It felt like she was floating in a virtual world, with no worries at all. This was the beginning of an addiction. In the beginning, it was a free addiction, as Smoke would supply the drugs. My mother would slowly yearn to chase the feeling of that first high. That decision to be vulnerable to a street substance would change our lives drastically.

My mother was always well put together. Pretty dark skin, and thick black hair, and her clothes were always on point. She thought she was in complete control of the new addiction because nothing had changed with our lifestyle during this time. She later found out that Smoke had a baby on the way with his side chick. My mother was hurt. That was the last straw. He denied it and claimed he was done messing with his side chick.

Smoke said things like, "You are my wife; no other woman matters." My mother had enough. She put him out and prayed to God to release the feelings she had for him. She prayed for closure. Unfortunately, now she had this addiction left behind that she would have to pay for herself. They were separated for a few months. Smoke begged to work on their marriage. My mother let him come back one night, and as he lay in their bed sound asleep, my mother looked at him with disgust.

"Wake up and get the fuck out!" she said in a firm voice.

He rubbed his eyes to remove the crust, "Why? What did I do? What happened, baby?" Smoke asked in a half-sleep crackling voice.

"I don't want you anymore. We are done. Get out!"

Smoke left in the middle of the night. The prayers to God had worked. She felt nothing for him. She no longer had the desire to fix her marriage. Smoke was gone, and Jazz was also gone, but unfortunately, the addiction stayed!

CHAPTER 6

WHEN YOU LEAST EXPECT IT

Time went on, and my mother dated a guy named Mr. Tim. Their connection was so unexpected. He lived across Dallas Court with his mother, Ms. Cassie. My mother and Mr. Tim were instant soul mates. It was the weirdest thing ever. It's like they loved each other before they ever met. They held hands in public and constantly kissed. They showed so much affection as if they were connected as one. I liked Mr. Tim, he was laid back and calm, but he had the look of a killer in his eyes. I knew my mother was safe with him. Sadly, they shared a common interest in their addiction; however, that didn't stop the genuine love they had for each other.

I liked Mr. Tim being around. It was my first time experiencing what true love was like for my mother. One thing I admired about Mr. Tim was how he didn't cross the line. He didn't try to be my father. He tried to build a personal relationship with me. For that, I gave him the utmost respect.

Although I cared for Mr. Tim, I missed my father dearly. My father was in and out of my life during these years. Not from lack of love or neglect, but more so from jail and life struggles. My father was never the same after losing his mother so young. Unfortunately, he had to figure out life challenges without the love and guidance of a parent. That's dangerous for a black man living in Baltimore. There was no question about whether he loved me or not. Three years could pass by without me seeing him, and I would hug and kiss him like he had left me the day before. I was a daddy's girl just as much as I was a mama's girl. The time apart didn't break our bond.

I guess my father could sense I missed him. My father unexpectedly came to pick me up with my brother Little Desmond Jr and Cameo. I loved my brothers so much. Little Desmond Jr looked just like me, and he was feminine like me too. My father would never admit it, but I always saw it. He wanted to be a girl; he wasn't into most boy things. He talked like a girl, walked like a girl, and gravitated toward girl activities. Weirdly enough, he still liked doing some boy things, like playing the Nintendo and wrestling with our baby brother Cameo.

I am my brother's keeper. My father took me to see my brother's mother, Les. I loved Les. She had spunk and a vibrant personality. I liked her Trinidadian culture and her Gemini ways. She was one unique woman. She loved me like I was her own, and that always felt good. Whenever I went to my brother's house, it was like my house. She didn't treat me any differently, and for that, she always held a special place in my heart. Les and my mother had a beautiful relationship as well. They would talk on the phone for hours when we were smaller.

The weekend was coming to an end, and my dad dropped me back off at my house. I was the last one to get dropped off. When my brothers got dropped off, they cried and told me how much they would miss me. I hugged them so tightly. I knew I would miss them. I felt so sad when I walked back to my house. I kept looking back at my father's car as he watched me walk up to my door. I thought, *I really love that man.* When I got in the house, my mother and Mr. Tim were in the kitchen eating spaghetti. My mom hugged me as if I had been gone for weeks. She told me how much she missed me and offered me some food. I wasn't hungry, but I loved my mother's spaghetti, so I let her make me a plate. As soon as I grabbed my fork, the phone rang. I started to get up to answer the phone, but my mother stopped me.

"No, baby, eat your food. I got it," my mother said.

"Ok," I said. I grabbed my fork and twirled the spaghetti noodles around and around before taking a big bite.

"Hello... What!" my mother roared. Shortly after, she dropped the phone and softly whimpered a cry.

I ran to her, "Oh My God! Mommy, what's wrong?" I asked.

"NO NO NO, not yet!" she screamed. She paced her body back and forth.

"Queen, what is it?" Mr. Tim asked as he walked over to her.

"It's my father. He passed away. Now I don't have a mother or a father. Not my daddy, please not my daddy," she cried loudly.

I began to cry. It killed me to see my mother in pain. My mother and I knew granddaddy was sick, but I didn't really comprehend how sick he was. I didn't understand I would lose him. I instantly felt empty. I thought, *here is that evil shadow hovering over my life, taking every piece of love I could ever endure to torture me.* Fucking death! It's back again. Now you want my Grandfather? My special granddaddy? He belongs to me. I need him. I LOVE HIM. He is the rock that holds this family together. You can't have him! But you can. You will have him, won't you? You win again. You are that powerful. You are death. We are all death. The moment we breathe life, we are already dying. This grief is yet another piece of my heart I'll never get back.

God won't give you more than you can handle, and if it's too much, he may send an angel to help you through. My mother was sad every day. I tried to stay strong for her, so I avoided talking about Granddaddy. My friends quickly became tired of hearing about it. I walked to school every day and talked to the crossing guard about Granddaddy. Although she was a stranger, it was so easy to talk to her, and she didn't mind.

Her name was Tricia. She had smooth dark skin, big gold earrings, and a gold front tooth; she wore red lipstick with black lip liner tracing her lips. I loved to watch her lips. I couldn't understand how she got the black liner to perfectly shape her lips. Every morning I would stand on the sidewalk and talk to her while she monitored the crosswalks. We'd talk until the school bell rang. I looked forward to our talks every morning. It was my therapy.

"Sunni, why don't you go to the playground with the other kids? Tricia asked as she walked the other kids across the street.

"I prefer to talk to you. I have no other adult to talk to like this."

"Little Ms. Sunni, you have an old soul. You would prefer to talk than run around like a crazy kid," she chuckled.

One afternoon, after school let out, Tricia said she wanted to walk me home. I didn't know why. Usually, when adults want to walk you home, you were in big trouble. After school, we walked to my house. I had to wait until Tricia made sure the last kid crossed the street safely. We walked to my house, and I asked my mother to come to the front door. My mother arrived at the front door with baking flour all over her hands from cooking. Her facial expression showed, *make this quick.*

"Hi, I'm Tricia, and I love your daughter," Tricia said in a blunt tone.

"You love her?" my mother asked with a confused look.

To break the awkwardness, I interrupted. "Ma, this is my crossing guard at school. Her name is Tricia. You know the one I told you I talk to every morning?" I reminded.

"Oh, nice to meet you," my mother said. Her body relaxed, and her face was more pleasant.

"I know you don't know me, but I want to be in Sunni's life forever. She is so special. Can I be her godmother?" Tricia asked gently.

My mother looked at me as if she wanted me to say something or explain who the heck this woman was and why I brought her there. I didn't speak; instead, I smiled and held Tricia's hand to give my approval. My mother agreed that Tricia could be my godmother. They chatted for a while, exchanged numbers, and ended with a hug. Tricia had one son, Squirrel. He was a few years younger than me. Tricia spoiled him, and he didn't want for anything. One weekend Tricia came to pick me up from my house, and we walked to Broadway Street. Broadway had clothing stores, markets, and boutiques. We walked into a shoe store; Squirrel and I started looking around.

"Baby, get whatever shoes you want," Tricia said to me.

"Any shoes I want?" I asked in disbelief.

"Yup, any shoes you want," she repeated.

"I'll take those fresh pair of K-Swiss, please." My face lit up with a huge smile. I almost fainted from the excitement.

"You can get two pairs. What else do you want?" Tricia asked.

"Are you sure, God Mommy? I don't want to spend all your money."

"You are so sweet, and that's why I love you. Nothing would make me happier," she assured me.

I asked for a pair of freaky Ree's (Reeboks), with the light baby blue Reebok sign. I hadn't had a pair of new shoes for a while. I wasn't a very materialistic person at this stage of my life, but I was grateful. There is no feeling like a new pair of kicks, especially two new pairs. I took off my old shoes and put them in the box my new K- Swiss came out of. I put on my fresh shoes and felt like a million bucks. I was sure to watch where I stepped to avoid messing them up. I felt good.

Tricia was in my life at the perfect time. God knew I needed her. Whenever my mother fell short, Tricia picked up with no complaints as a true godmother would. I went with my beautiful godmother every other weekend, and she was the empty piece of love I needed in that period of my life. She couldn't replace Granddaddy's love, but she kept his spot in my heart warm. Shortly after Granddaddy died, Mr. Tim was arrested for drugs, which pushed my mother over the edge.

My mother was in full addiction mode after losing her father and now her soul mate. The pain of losing her father was more than she could bear. This new habit became a way for her to escape her reality. I didn't realize it at the time, but God always showed up in my life at the right time. He never left me. No matter how alone I felt, he was always there. My escape was my beautiful godmother. God sent me an angel named Tricia when I least expected it.

Addiction is something we all suffer from in one way or another. Some people are addicted to food, sex, money, plastic surgery, street drugs, prescription drugs, alcohol, pornography, shopping, working, or even going to the gym. No one is immune to life's bullshit. We must constantly outsmart addiction. It's a constant battle to be strong enough to put that muffin down or to avoid the vending machine at work. Some of us are addicted to our abusive spouses. No matter how hard we try to leave him or her, we answer the phone every time they call. Some people are workaholics. They're addicted to working to avoid dealing with their personal life outside of work.

All addictions sneak up on you, and we always feel we have the habit under control until we wake up one day high as Fat Charles' Ass. Or maybe, we wake up 300 pounds because we couldn't control ourselves from picking up yet another muffin. The gym freaks have addictions as well. They become so obsessed with their body image that they put the gym before having a social life. They become so infatuated with the gym; all they talk about are calories, meal plans, lifting, and their size. They literally lose their personalities.

We all use different addictions in life to feel better and to deal with our many issues. Most of the time, we can't kick the habit until we fix the issue within us. We must dig deep and get to the root cause of why we are becoming dependent on that specific habit. It's easy to blame the world. It's always someone else's fault, but listen to this; it's so much easier to blame yourself. Then you can start to heal. Then you can recognize it was you who went from casually getting high into full addiction mode. Life can knock you down when you least expect it. Life can drag you through the terrors of hell. That's where my Queen and I are headed. We are headed towards a life cycle of addiction and pain.

CHAPTER 7

TIME TO MOVE ON

Now I was starting to feel myself. I started smoking cigarettes to fit in. Although cigarettes stink and made me stink, I still smoked them. Luckily, I only smoked them on occasion and was able to drop the habit before I got fully addicted. I felt cool smoking, which was ridiculous because I had asthma. That was the weak side of me coming out. I was never really a follower, but I was genuinely lost. I didn't know where I fit in. I was hood, but not ghetto. I was fun, but not wild. I was flirty but not having sex.

No matter what people may think, the projects were a fun place to grow up in the early '90s. Yes, there was violence and drugs; however, there were life lessons, good and bad, that would ultimately prepare you for life. Every day was an adventure, whether we went to a dance competition over West Baltimore or flirt with the boys in another project in East Baltimore. Some of us were in the marching band called "New Edition." Our motto song was something like...

"New Edition, there's no competition
Believe it or not, cause we're not superstitious
Beating on drums, yeah, we're number one
In case you didn't know, we're just having fun!"

Even the walk to Flag House projects for some Chinese food was an adventure. Flag House had the best Chinese food, but it could sometimes cause conflict. The people in the two neighboring projects didn't always like each other. It was weird because the two projects were so close together, within walking distance. Flag House had high-rise and low-rise buildings. I stayed out of the project's drama. I went where I wanted to go, and I got along with most of the flag house girls, and I thought their boys were cute. We only lived 10 minutes from the Baltimore Inner Harbor, so we could walk and get free entertainment any day of the week. We always had something to do, but there was always just as much drama as it was fun.

So, I wanted to act grown, huh? I was with a group of friends, well they were more like associates. We strolled through the projects as they scraped up a few dollars to get a nickel bag of weed. If you asked five drug dealers for $1, that would be enough to get high. Although I sometimes found myself in these little clicks, I didn't smoke weed. It was fun just walking around.

"Are you trying to smoke? Can you buy the blunt?" Sammy asked me.

"Ok, cool. I'll get the blunt," I quickly responded before realizing what I agreed to. I thought to myself, *oh shit, you're about to smoke weed.* I was scared but couldn't back out now. The peer pressure was on, and I felt like all eyes were on me. We walked to the corner store in Herring Court, and I bought two Phillies Blunts.

"Roll up Sunni," Sammy demanded.

"Sammy, I don't know how to roll," I confessed.

"What? Girl, stop playing. How you live in the jets, and you don't know how to roll?" she sarcastically asked.

I gave her the *I'm not playing* look. She sucked her teeth as if she was annoyed. She reached her hand out to get the blunts. She then cracked the blunt paper with her nails and started breaking (crumbling) up the weed. I watched Sammy lick the blunt repeatedly. I took mental notes so I could learn how to roll.

She took the lighter and burned the blunt to dry her spit. I thought *this is some nasty shit to smoke someone else's saliva, but whatever.* She then ripped off the tip and threw it to the ground, and lit the blunt. I had been around weed plenty of times, so it wasn't a new smell, but I had never smoked it, so it smelled new this time. We often ignore the things we don't do, because it doesn't affect us. Sammy handed me the blunt. I took a puff and blew it back out.

"Girl, you didn't inhale it! You are wasting the weed. Let me show you how to smoke," Sammy yelled.

"I did inhale it!" I screamed in a defensive tone.

"Let me show you," Sammy said. She took it out of my hand and showed me how to inhale. I took it back from her hand and sucked it in, and held it in as she showed me. Here I was, 11 years old, smoking my first blunt. I passed the blunt to Fats.

"Your bluffing ass," Fats laughed as she took the blunt out of my hand.

"Shut up, Fats," I lightly pushed her arm.

"This shit smells good, right?" Fats asked as she inhaled the smoke. The other girls agreed by nodding their heads.

Fats and I became cool over the years, and we never mentioned the little childhood fights we had when I first moved into the Projects. We always seemed to get into minor arguments here and there, but nothing heavy. Fats loved my mother, and I loved hers. It's probably what kept us around each other so much. I called her mother Aunt Resa, and she called my mother, Aunt Queen. Aunt Resa was my baby, and I would do anything for her.

The weed was kicking in, and I felt super strange. Everything was so loud. It was like the people around me were screaming. I heard all the car engines riding by, all the different music coming from each person's house, the ice cream truck, and all the kids yelling for a dollar. I was so alert and paranoid. There was so much chaos going on in my mind.

"I need to lie down," I said with no warning. I stopped walking. My feet came to an abrupt stop.

"What do you mean, lay where? You are tripping!" Sammy expressed.

"Don't start geeking and have Aunt Queen on our ass," Fats said as she laughed and shook her head.

I ignored them. I lay on the concrete steps and looked at the sky. It was beautiful! I had never admired the sky like that before. I was high as hell! I watched every cloud move and pointed out the different images that I could see. I talked to Jazz, Granddaddy, my grandmother, and even Toni. I could hear all the conversations in the surrounding background. Although I could hear them, I wasn't listening. I was at peace. I was relaxed. I could've looked at the sky for hours. I talked to GOD about everything. My fears, my life, my dreams, and my anger over the people I lost. Then suddenly, someone slapped my leg and broke my peace.

"Get your high ass up off this ground!" Sammy hollered with frowned eyebrows, and she seemed annoyed.

"No, leave me here. I'll see you all later," I said. I brushed them off, and I continued to look up at the sky.

"I told y'all we shouldn't have smoked with her. Now she is acting nuts," Fats pointed out. She shook her head and walked off. I ignored her, and they left me on the ground.

"Finally, I'm alone," I said aloud. I sat there for what felt like hours, but it had only been about twenty minutes. I finally got up when a lady was trying to come out of her door, which I had blocked with my entire body stretched out on the hard concrete.

"Baby, you good?" the woman asked.

"Yes, ma'am. Thanks."

"Okay then, you shouldn't be laying out here on this concrete like this. What court you live in?"

"I'm good, I promise. I was just admiring the sky."

I walked away before she could say anything else. Time got away from me. I felt like I was in another world. The projects had never looked so pretty. It was the first time I acknowledged how much grass surrounded the concrete. I roamed the Projects for a couple of hours alone until I ran into Sweets.

"Twin, what the hell is wrong with you?" Sweets immediately asked.

"I smoked, and I feel crazy as shit. How can I make this feeling go away?" I asked.

"Your ass is high!" she laughed.

"How do I look?" I asked in a shaky voice.

"DUMB!" She quickly responded.

We both burst out laughing. Sweets had already smoked weed. It was like a tradition in her family. Her entire family smoked, even her Grammy. When Sweets and I were about seven years old, we tried to smoke salt and pepper rolled in notebook paper. We pretended we were smoking weed and the notebook paper was "Top" paper. We coughed and sneezed from the pepper for hours. It was stupid, but it was fun.

I went home after a while because I wanted the high to go away. I wanted to lie down or sleep it off. I tried to open my front door; it was locked, and I didn't have my key. During this time, people would be in and out of our house. The drug traffic was out of control. I knocked on the door with irritation, and my mother came to the door. My mother was beautiful, absolutely breathtaking. I remember thinking, *damn, she is gorgeous.* I mean, she always looked beautiful, but while I was high, she was even more attractive. Soon as she opened the door, she wasted no time questioning me.

"What the hell is wrong with your eyes?" my mother asked.

I looked her in her eyes, "The same thing that's wrong with yours!" I quickly responded.

Usually, that type of smart comment would've been a guaranteed smack, but this time facts were facts. We were both high. I didn't play with my mother. I gave her the utmost respect. My mother demanded respect from everyone no matter what she was doing. She always kept herself up, even during addiction. My mother never left the house without her hair done, and every strand had to be in place. Her clothes were ironed, and her makeup beat. She was always discreet around me. We had many heart-to-heart talks about her getting help. My mother and I shared everything. A mother should never be ashamed of what life throws at her or hide the truth about life's struggles from her child. Honesty kept our bond strong, but love made our bond unbreakable.

When it's time to move on, it's time to move on, whether you are ready or not! It was a pretty spring night. I was outside with Sweets playing jacks. We loved to play jacks. I usually kicked her butt, but this time she beat me, and she kept bragging. It annoyed me, so I went home, and Sweets went into her aunt's house. I cut on the TV, and I was so happy to see the show, "Martin" was on. I popped popcorn and got prepared to laugh my heart out. I was also delighted that the house was empty. I watched the episode of "Martin," when Martin thought someone stole his CD player. I laughed so hard at him acting like Nino Brown. I went to the kitchen to get some water while the commercials were on. Just as I was about to sit down, I heard a knock at the door.

"Who is it?" I yelled from the top of the steps. They didn't respond but knocked again.

I thought, *fuck them! It's probably somebody trying to get high. My mother is not here anyway, so fuck it.* Back to the sofa, I go. I heard, BOOM, BOOM, BOOM! My heart raced instantly. I listened to the front door drop. I threw the popcorn up in the air.

"GET ON THE FUCKING FLOOR, GET THE FUCK ON THE FLOOR!" the cops yelled.

It paralyzed me. I couldn't move. There were cops everywhere and guns with red lights on my chest. I put my hands up, but I didn't get on the floor. The red light on my chest scared me to the point I was afraid to move. I could not move. I thought if I moved, the red light might make a mistake and shoot me.

"FOR THE LAST TIME, GET ON THE FUCKING FLOOR!" a cop yelled.

Tears rolled down my cheeks, and I slowly went down. Soon as I was down on the floor, they checked me and asked me; *what's my name? Who is in the house? Where is Queen? Where are the drugs? Where is the money? Where are the guns?*

"I don't know. I don't know, I DON'T KNOW!" I repeatedly replied.

They started destroying the house. I mean, they really ruined the house. They ripped up the sofa, threw all the food out of the kitchen cabinets, flipped over all the chairs, and destroyed all the bedrooms. I watched in amazement and disgust as they destroyed our belongings. The cops constant yelling made me nervous. Their lack of recognition of me being a child made me angry.

A White cop came over with a portrait of my mother that an artist had drawn of her.

"Who is this to you?" he shoved the portrait in my face.

"That's my mother," I mumbled.

"Queen?" he rudely asked as if he didn't already know the answer.

"Yes," I answered with no emotion.

"I will not keep playing these fucking games with you, little girl. Where is your mother?" he asked with aggression.

"Get the FUCK out of my face! I don't know anything!" I screamed. I cried hysterically.

"Come on, Tom, she's just a child," a black cop said as he walked over towards us.

I forgot about the guns for a split second, nor did I care about the police authority. I held my tears as long as I could. I was so tired of them disrespecting me. I wanted them out of my house and out of my face. I no longer cared about my life. I thought, *who were they to treat me this way? I am a child. I'm a pretty traumatized child at that, yet they decided to point guns at me and curse at me? NO! I'm Sunni. I don't take shit from anyone! Especially when they are coming for MY QUEEN, so fuck these disrespectful cops.*

I remembered a movie I watched that said: "You have the right to remain silent." I begin to imitate that movie, so I said nothing. I answered nothing. They got nothing. My silence annoyed the cops. They got bored and threatened to take me to foster care, and I would never see my mother again. I continued to say NOTHING. I cried in silence. Just the thought of losing my mother was killing me on the inside. Eventually, they let me go outside. I tried to go to my neighbor's house, but a cop stopped me by holding his arm out.

"No, we have to call social services for you," the angry cop said.

"No, I'll take her," my neighbor Bea intervened.

"You are not her family, so you can't take her," the cop barked.

"Please call my Aunt Shelby. She will get here before social services. Please, Bea. Her number is 233-XXXX," I yelled over the cop's shoulder to Bea. The cop's strong arm prevented me from moving any further.

"No one answered the phone. Do you have another number?" Bea asked.

"Please keep calling. I have no one else," I pleaded as the panic about my aunt not being home begin to overwhelm my thoughts.

The third call and finally, my Aunt Shelby answered. When Bea said, "Hello." I instantly felt a sense of relief. Bea briefly told my Aunt Shelby what happened, and my aunt said she was on her way. The officer said he had to speak to her before he called child protective service. He asked my aunt a series of questions. I asked the cop multiple times if I could go into the house to get some of my things. He repeatedly told me no. It seemed like my Aunt Shelby took forever to get there. Finally, I looked up and saw my aunt, uncle Lee, Diamond, and Darin. I ran to them and cried my heart out. My aunt held me.

"It's okay, Sunni. I'm here now," Aunt Shelby said.

"Thank you for coming. They were going to send me to foster care," I cried.

She gave the cops a piece of her mind for treating me so poorly. One cop finally allowed us to go into the house with him to get some of my belongings. I looked around at my destroyed house and thought of all the memories we made there. I knew it was over. I knew I would never step foot in those rooms again. Once a house is raided, they evict you from public housing. I went to my bedroom and sobbed. I grabbed a few of my favorite books, some undies, a few pictures, and whatever I could carry while the cop reminded me to hurry.

So, I left my home with one bookbag and a plastic bag full of my past life. It was time to move on. I was devastated and angry. I worried deeply for my mother. I didn't want her on the run or in any kind of trouble. My mother was strong but sensitive, just like me. Now I had to take the walk of shame to my aunt's car.

Everyone was staring, talking, and gossiping. Saying things like, *"Queen's house got raided, Sunni was in there alone; people are going to take all their stuff, them boys kicked that joint in!"* They couldn't wait to talk. I was humiliated and grew a strong hate towards the cops. I didn't trust the police. I thought they were evil and cold. Even the ones who tried to be decent were bad in my eyes. I put them all in a category together, far as I was concerned, fuck the police. As I walked to the car, I saw Sweets crying. She ran and hugged me.

"Twin, I'm so sorry. What will I do without you?" Sweets asked with heavy eyes filled with tears.

"I will always love you, Sweets. Stay healthy, okay. If you see my mother, tell her I'm with my aunt, and I'm safe. Call me anytime. My aunt's number is 233-XXXX, " I cried and squeezed her tight.

I sat in the back seat of my aunt's car and looked around at my hood. I reminisced on everything and became sadder. I had butterflies in my gut, and I felt so uneasy. I thought about the first time I stood on my front steps when I was only four years old. I remember I thought to myself, *what is this place?* I now knew what that place was; it was my hood, it was all of our HOOD, it was my home, it was the Projects. Goodbye Perkins, it's time to move on...

CHAPTER 8

REGARDLESS

I moved in with my Aunt Shelby after the house raid. The first night was hell! I cried nonstop. From the very first day I was born, Aunt Shelby loved me like one of her own children. She tried to make me feel as comfortable as possible in this unexpected situation. I wasn't comfortable, though. I missed my house, my bed, my room, and especially my mother. You never know what you have until it's gone. Diamond had her own room. Darin and Baby D shared a room. By now, Aunt Shelby had three kids. We called her youngest son Baby D.

Uncle Lee told me I could sleep wherever I wanted, and this was my house too. I didn't know where I wanted to sleep. I felt like a burden. My mom called at 3 o'clock that morning and said she was okay, and she was staying at a neighbor's house. I was so relieved to hear her voice, but I was also upset with her. She told me I would have to stay with Aunt Shelby for a while, and she was so sorry this happened. We cried on the phone for about an hour. My mother and I had never been apart. I would have preferred to live in a shoe with her than to be without her. She was my balance, she was my best friend, and she was my Queen.

Diamond was the only girl in the house besides Aunt Shelby. Being in charge was *her* normal before I arrived. She had her room, and she never had to share her space with anyone, which was understandable. She had a daybed in her room, which is what I slept on. Gosh, was she serious about her daybed. The pillows had to be set up neatly and in a specific order. Before I could barely open my eyes in the morning, she would already be up telling me how to make up the daybed and how to put the pillows back in the order she had them. She would then leave the room to take her routine morning shower. Soon as she would leave, I would say to myself, *fuck these pillows and fuck this daybed.* I loved to curse amongst myself.

Cursing was fun, and it allowed me to express my frustrations. I never disrespected any adults out loud, I was a very respectful child, but the thoughts in my mind were not. What they didn't know is that I would surely curse them out in my head. I would say things to myself like, *Oh please shut the fuck up, Got damn, you nagging again woman, somebody, please get this bitch, blah blah blah I'm still not doing shit, this man talks too fucking much, shit her breath stink, here this mother fucker go running his mouth!* I'd sometimes make a mistake and laugh out loud at my ignorant cursing sprees that played in my mind.

Diamond and I were like sisters, so we argued like siblings. I truly loved and admired her, but she got on my damn nerves. I'm sure I got on hers too. She was clean, disciplined, and set in her ways. I could've learned a lot from her superb habits, like the fact she immediately made up her bed the moment she woke up. Instead, I was annoyed by her antics. I was carefree and didn't give two shits about where the pillows should be placed on a bed, nor did I care about making up a bed at the crack of dawn.

It's one thing to come over for a few days in the summer, but it was a totally different experience moving in permanently. I looked at Aunt Shelby's kids as if they were spoiled. They had everything! Diamond had hush puppies shoes, Timberland boots, and name-brand clothes. She often went to the hairdressers or my other Aunt Harriet to get her hair permed and wrapped. Darin got his hair braided every week, and Baby D had every Nintendo and Sega Genesis game on the market. Aunt Shelby worked her butt off to keep her kids happy. I watched her care for everyone except herself. I didn't like that. She worked, she cooked, she cleaned, she bought everything, and she never complained. Uncle Lee was a hard worker too, and he contributed his money to the household as the provider should. Aunt Shelby still did most of the housework alone. That annoyed me.

I was overprotective of my Aunt Shelby. She wasn't just an aunt; she was my second mother. I would spend as much time with her as possible. We'd go to the thrift store and eat lunch after. I loved those moments. We would play monopoly together as a family, and whoever lost would have to clean up all the pieces after we threw them up in the air. Aunt Shelby would "play school" with us, she would be the teacher, and we would be the students. She randomly took us for long rides to the county, just to visit a park where we could play and run wild.

You can take a person out of the hood, but you can't take the hood out of the person. Living at Aunt Shelby's was so different from how I was used to living. I was street-smart. There was nothing I didn't know about the streets. I happened to be book-smart too. Not as book-smart as Diamond, but I had pretty good grades also. At Aunt Shelby's, there was no pressure to fit into a particular category. I could just be ME. Diamond attended West Baltimore Middle School. Aunt

Shelby got me registered at the elementary school, Samuel F B Morse 98. I started the 5th grade in the middle of the school year. No one liked me at the new school.

South Baltimore was a mixed community. The Black girls dated the White guys, and the Black guys loved the White girls. Aunt Shelby lived on a laid-back street with other homeowners and honest working people. Just one block over was consumed with crime and prostitution. As the neighborhood started going down, the other neighborhood streets became overpopulated with Section 8 voucher holders. The kids at the school I attended were about 50% Black, 40% White, and 10% mixed. The 40% White kids were just as ghetto, if not more than the black kids. This environment was weird for me.

There were a group of girls who bussed to the school from Baltimore Street. They immediately decided they didn't like me. So, here's the deal. Yes, I was from Perkins Projects, and yes, I fought a lot when necessary, but truth be told, I didn't like conflict. I learned to adapt to my environment no matter where I was. I would survive by any means necessary. I would fight to protect myself by any means necessary, but why was it always necessary?

The beautiful spirit inside of me was sweet, sensitive, and happy. I was no angel, and I had a slick mouth for sure, but my heart was too big for this world. Life was sucking the joy out of my little soul. I fought to save myself. I fought with my inner demons not to let life change the good person I was. Every traumatic situation took another little piece of me, another little part of my innocence. At this point, I was mentally in a bad place. I missed my mother and lost contact with my father (again). I missed Honey and Sweets. To top it off, my Godmother's phone was disconnected, and I had no other way to get in contact with her.

I walked up to the school doors just as the bell rang. The leader of the group name was Shanny. She disliked me the most. Shanny was unattractive, slim, dark, and looked like a boy. She dressed like a girl but looked like a boy in the face. Her clothes were too big as if she wore hand-me-downs. I grabbed the door handle in a rush because I just heard the doorbell ring, and I wanted to avoid being late.

"Use another door," Shanny said in a serious voice.

"No thanks, I'm going to use this door," I said. I proceeded to grab the door handle. I thought to myself, *who the fuck does she think she is?*

Her friend came from behind Shanny and stood on the side of her, "Like she said, use another door!"

I rolled my eyes. I thought, *let me just bite the bullet on this one and use the other door since it's two of them.* I knew when to put my pride aside and take a hit to my ego. I also knew it was too early in the morning to be getting jumped. I walked to the other door, where another girl stood. I proceeded to grab that door handle.

"Nope, not this door either Bitch!" The 3rd girl said with a smirk that showed her brutally yellow teeth.

As I took a deep breath and mentally prepared to get jumped by these three girls, I told myself, *I'm walking through one of these doors. I'm done playing with these bitches.* My next thought was, *who to hit first?* I looked around my surroundings for a stick or some type of weapon, and I found nothing. Just as I started to walk up to the leader Shanny, a teacher came out of her classroom.

"What's the problem?" the teacher asked with a look of concern.

"No problem, right light skin?" Shanny looked at me with an evil smirk on her face.

"Nope, no problem, I was just about to walk through this door REGARDLESS," I said to the teacher with no emotion.

That was my way of letting them know that I was coming through the door, whether we had to fight or not. That statement was my 1st mistake. It was the beginning of hell for me at that school. What I didn't know was that Shanny had five brothers and three sisters, and a massive amount of cousins. Her dirty family pretty much ran the school.

I wondered, *did her family have kids for a living. Why the hell would an entire family decide to have a baby every year?* I assumed fighting all her brothers made her a beast and her unattractive face made her angry. She bullied everyone, and everyone kissed her ass. I got to the cafeteria that day and watched her beat up a little boy like she was a grown man. She stomped him, spit on him, and dragged him until the principal came. As the principal walked her out, she stopped and smiled at me.

"I do this for fun! REGARDLESS!" Shanny said to me. She looked at her busted knuckles and grinned. I looked her right in her eyes and smiled, but I said nothing. I will never show fear. I thought, *fuck her and that pussy little boy she beat up.* I glanced at her knuckles and turned my head. There was a random thick girl who sat next to me at the cafeteria table. She ate extremely fast and sloppy. For some reason, she thought I was interested in her opinion.

"You better fix it with her. Shanny will never stop, I'm telling you," the thick girl said as ketchup came out of the side of her mouth.

"I'm Sunni, and I DON'T kiss nobody's ass. So she can keep right on coming."

That statement was my 2nd mistake. Girls love to gossip. The random thick girl wasted no time reporting back to Shanny. I got home that day and waited for Aunt Shelby. I wanted to make her aware that school was hell for me, and that I may get suspended for fighting. I didn't want to be the problem child in her house. I wanted her to know that it was out of my control because they were coming for me, and they wanted blood. The phone rang, and I answered. It was my Queen. For some reason, I instantly felt nervous. My heart was beating fast, and I felt a little sweat on my forehead. I listened carefully to hear the tone of her voice. I thought, *is she okay? Why is her voice breaking? Should I be worried?*

"Sunni, I know things have been hard on us, but God loves us, and we will make it through anything with faith and love. I must go away for a while," she said in a slow deep voice.

"I figured that, Mommy. I know God loves us, but why must everything be so hard?" I questioned.

"It's life and also some bad choices. It's not a choice for me to be away from you, but it must be done. Stay strong and continue to be the bright Sunni that I know you are."

"Ma, I love you, and I will be strong, but this is hard on me. I know, in the end, this will be a blessing. I love you and call me soon."

I quickly hung up the phone to avoid bursting into tears. This news wasn't what I needed. It made me weak. I became depressed. I started crying all the time. I cried so much I drove myself crazy. I stayed in a small bubble at home, and at school, I was miserable. The phone call distracted me, and by the time Aunt Shelby came home, I didn't want to talk about school anymore.

Shanny got suspended from school because of the fight she had in the cafeteria with the little boy. When she returned, I guess she didn't want to fight me right away. She probably wanted to avoid another suspension. A few weeks went by, and things seemed to calm down. NOT! Lesson #1, never sleep on an envious chick. Lesson #2, handle conflict the moment it happens, don't wait for the fight to come to you. Go to the fight. Lesson #3, when it's more than one person coming for you, chose the leader and swing until your arms can't move.

School let out, and all the bus kids were walking to the buses. All the walkers were walking home. I was walking alone eating some candy in la-la land, daydreaming about what I would eat when I got to the house. I was interrupted from my thoughts when I heard someone yell, "REGARDLESS!" I turned around, and I saw all the buses leaving, but Shanny and her crew were not on the buses; instead, they were walking towards me. I thought, *FUCK! These ugly bitches never give up!*

My mind started racing, my heart was pumping out of my chest, and the intense butterflies in my gut were paralyzing. I told myself, *I'm definitely not about to run. I can't talk my way out of this one. I can't beat five ugly beasts, so all I can do is remember who I am. I am Sunni! I am strong! I have been through more than the average! I am Queen's daughter, and I don't run.* Shanny and her crew were getting closer, so I dropped my book bag and put my hands up in a fighting position. Soon as they got close enough, I immediately hit Shanny in the eye and swung for dear life. With every blow I swung, I cried, not from fear, but anger. I felt blows coming from everywhere. It felt more like I was fighting ten girls.

"Break it up. Break it up!" the counselor, Mrs. Shaw, screamed.

Other neighborhood adults assisted with breaking up the fight as well.

"BITCH, it's not over! You lucky they came, watch, watch, watch!" Shanny and her crew yelled.

I remained silent and watched people hold them back. I felt my face to see what damage had been done. I felt nothing. I felt my hair out of place. I took my hands and rolled my hair back; I removed the ponytail holder, and I felt just a few strands of hair coming out. I tasted this bitter taste in my mouth. It was blood. My lip was busted. I licked my lips and spat the blood on the ground toward Shanny and her crew. I grabbed my bookbag off the ground.

"REGARDLESS!" I shouted.

I walked away with my busted lip and my pride. In my mind, they were weak. They didn't even get me on the ground. I stood up on my own two feet the entire fight. Where I'm from, that's a win! As I continued to walk away, I could hear them yelling angry remarks in the background as the adults pulled them back towards the school. I walked home slowly and felt a strong sense of relief. I didn't care my lip was busted, I handled myself, and they knew I wasn't afraid, so that's all that mattered. I also felt like I had a therapy session because the fight released a lot of anger I held inside since the house raid.

Aunt Shelby was furious, not at me, but at the fact, someone put their hands on me. I lied and told my family I was only fighting Shanny. My aunt would've been devastated to know multiple girls were fighting me, and Diamond would have been at my school ready to kill. Diamond was pissed that I had a busted lip, so I couldn't tell her it was more than one girl. I was her little sister, and as much as I annoyed her, she didn't play about me. I had to talk her out of coming to the school for just Shanny. I didn't want her to get in any trouble; she was a good girl. I would've felt like crap involving her in a violent situation, so I just lied.

God is working again. He is sending me yet another Angel, and this time her name is Mrs. Shaw. The next day, I saw the school counselor Mrs. Shaw. She called me to her office as soon as I got to my first-period class. I didn't get suspended because we were not inside the school when the fight took place. Mrs. Shaw was a heavyset, tall woman with dreads and a huge butt.

"What happened yesterday, Sunni?" she asked.

"They just don't like me," I answered in a calm tone.

"I like you. You seem to be a sweet girl. Why do you have so much sadness in your eyes? What's really going on?" she questioned.

"My mother is gone away, I lost contact with my father, I can't reach my godmother, I miss my best friend Sweets like crazy, and I haven't talked to my sister Honey in weeks," I released a sigh.

"You have a lot built up. I'll make a deal with you. No more fighting, and I'll take you to see your mother," Mrs. Shaw offered with optimism.

My face lit up! I was so excited! I came to Mrs. Shaw's office every day to talk about my life. It felt good, and it got me out of my depression state. As promised, Mrs. Shaw took me to see my mother, and I was so happy to lay eyes on my Queen. I looked at her beautiful milky dark skin, and I wanted to grab her and keep her with me forever. We had an amazing time. I was sad to leave her, but seeing her was what I needed to stay strong. I will never forget Mrs. Shaw for stepping in and talking me off the ledge.

As for Shanny and her crew, they found a new victim. I was no longer fun for them because they knew I was a challenge. I went out of my way to look them up and down whenever we crossed paths. Instead of avoiding them, I walked towards them. Fear is only in our minds, it's not real, and it doesn't exist. We create our own fear; it's not a natural balance of the universe. Fear is something we torture ourselves with to stay comfortable. To conquer fear, we must face it, or we can never move forward. If we avoid facing fear, we become weak, and I'm no weak Bitch REGARDLESS.

CHAPTER 9

MY CHICO

God shows up and shows out. My Queen is back! Mrs. Shaw kept her promise and helped us get an apartment. We moved to Frederick Ave, the area known as F&T, which stood for Frederick and Tremont. We had a lovely apartment with hardwood floors and a balcony. I had a huge room with a walk-in closet. The place was nice. It was a massive upgrade from the small rooms in the projects, but we never stayed home. It was too quiet on Frederick Ave. We ran back to Perkins every chance we got. I would also catch the bus to Westside Shopping Center to walk over to my Aunt Shelby's house. I missed them.

By this time, my father finally found me. He came to our new place a week after we moved in. He rang the doorbell. I opened the door and jumped in his arms. It was so good to see my father and hug his manly arms. He took me shopping for new clothes. He gave me multiple phone numbers to reach him so that we wouldn't lose contact again. We hung out the entire weekend. He treated me like a two-year-old, and I let him. I enjoyed being daddy's little girl. My mother and I constantly traveled back to Perkins. The decision to go back to Perkins so often wasn't a good idea for either one of us. Old environments can bring back old habits.

I had a friend named Nikki, who I met around F&T. She was from another part of West Baltimore; she lived in Edmondson Village. Nikki was two years older than me and much more developed. She had big boobs and slanted eyes. We had instant chemistry. My mother went to Perkins for the weekend, and for the first time, I didn't want to go. I asked if I could stay over at Nikki's house instead.

My mother agreed after speaking to Nikki's mother. I was so excited. Nikki said there was a dope party up the "Village," also known as Edmondson Village. Nikki and her stepfather picked me up in his car, and we rode back to her neighborhood. The houses were so big. The guys seemed to be more relaxed than the guys from Perkins. I observed everything about her hood.

We were showering and getting dressed to go to the party. I had a yellow "Boss" Shirt and a black "Boss" skirt. My father bought me the outfit the week prior. I dropped the iron on my shirt by mistake, which created a giant iron print in the middle of the shirt. I was so upset. I was even more annoyed that I didn't have a backup outfit. Nikki convinced me it would be dark, and no one would see it.

I was still pissed, and I thought, *how will no one notice a bright yellow shirt with an iron print?* I had been to many house parties, but this was a new hood and a new crowd. I was a little nervous. We got to the party, and the club music was jumping on a big gray radio. The same few songs were playing until the cassette guy came with more music.

Nikki and I were laughing and talking. Suddenly, I could feel someone looking at me. The feeling was so intense. I stopped talking and looked up. I saw the most handsome guy I had ever seen in my life. He was gorgeous. He was perfect in every way possible. He had milky brown skin, dark shiny, thick eyebrows, and bright, glassy eyes. He had six cornrows, which didn't look freshly done, but it didn't matter because he had a nice grain of hair. We stared at each other for what felt like hours. Finally, he smiled at me, and I smiled back. Neither one of us wanted to turn away. I turned my head first. When I turned around, Nikki was dead smack in my face.

"What the hell was that about?" she asked with her eyebrows raised.

"What?" I asked innocently.

"You and Little Chico were staring at each other like you in a damn soap opera."

"Oh, so his name is Chico?" I asked before I laughed at her soap opera comment.

"Yes, he's a cutie, right?" she asked.

"Cute is an understatement. He's gorgeous," I said with lust in my eyes.

I asked Nikki a million questions about Chico. I could tell she was getting annoyed and wanted to enjoy the party, but I didn't care. I wanted Chico, and I needed as much information as possible. I asked, does he have a girlfriend? Where is he from? Who is that boy next to him? Is that his twin? I asked the questions faster than my lips could move. Finally, Nikki told me to talk to him. She grabbed my arm, pulling me in his direction.

"No, Nikki, Let me go. I don't want to talk to him," I explained.

"You sure? You sure did have a lot of questions a few seconds ago," she sarcastically stated.

"Girl, chill, I promise I won't ask anything else," I lied.

"Your scared ass," she laughed and let my arm go. I was afraid she would pull me over to Chico and embarrass me, so I shut up.

A guy grabbed my waist to dance. It was dark, and I swayed my hips from side-to-side dancing to the beat. I didn't even bother to look back to see what the guy looked like, but I felt him growing an erection. All I knew about this guy was that he wasn't Chico. Chico was across the room, looking me dead in my eyes as I danced with this mystery guy. I danced more sexually now that I had Chico's attention. He stared intensely. The music had switched to more of a 90's remix.

"Oh shit, that's my song!" I screamed to Nikki.

I walked away from the random guy and started dancing and singing along. I sang Mary J Blige, "Real Love." A girl walked up and freaked Chico. I instantly became jealous. His boys were joking and laughing, saying, "Little Chico, you can't handle that!" Referring to the bold girl who took him and danced aggressively, pumping her ass hard against his man piece. He lost focus of me, and now he was watching her butt rub against his penis. He smiled and held his hands up and let her take control. I thought, *he's even cuter when he smiles, and she's a slutty, trampy thirst bucket.* The night went on, Nikki and I had a ball; we danced until we got sweaty.

"I'll be back, Boo. I'm going to the bathroom," I yelled in Nikki's ear.

"Okay. Don't sit on the toilet," Nikki laughed.

"Girl, shut up. I learned that in Pre-K," I stated. As I walked up the basement steps, someone grabbed my arm from behind.

"You leaving without dancing with me?" Chico asked.

I turned around and looked him dead in his eyes.

"I don't like to be the last dance," I sarcastically answered. I continued to walk up the steps.

He grabbed me more aggressively and whispered in my ear with a soft tone, "But I saved the best for last."

"You know that was corny, right?" I asked as I tried to hold back from laughing in his face.

"Yeah, I know. The moment it came out of my mouth, I knew it was corny as shit," Chico confessed.

We both burst into laughter because we knew his response was cheesy. Usher's song, "Nice and Slow," was playing. This was the first slow song all night, which let us know the party was coming to an end. We danced slowly and intimately. We danced like we were the only two people in the room. I enjoyed every second, his body heat was warm, and his neck smelled good. Usher was singing, "They call me U S H E R - R A Y M O N D." I sang along, spelling his name out as if I was him.

"You think you can sing, huh?" Chico asked with a slight smirk.

"Nope, but I still do it," I admitted.

"You have a really pretty smile," he said as we faced each other.

"Come on, girl! People are leaving," Nikki interrupted.

"I'm coming, Nikki dag," I yelled with frustration. She acted like she had something to do. I slowly let Chico go.

"Wait, I don't even know your name," he said as if he was worried I would disappear at that very moment.

"It's cool. I know your name is Chico. That's all that matters," I said.

I walked outside to catch up with Nikki, who was watching me with an annoyed facial expression.

"Can you please tell me your name before you go?" Chico insisted.

"Hi, I'm Sunni," I extended my hand to him for a formal handshake.

He jokingly kissed my hand as if I was royalty. I realized at that moment; he was silly but gentle. He wasn't a thug. He was goofy. We talked for about five minutes then he gave me his number. Chico and his boys walked one way, and Nikki and I walked the opposite way. I looked back a few times, and he did too. I caught him looking. I talked Nikki's head off about him the entire night.

I kept replaying our dance—the way he grabbed my arm and how bright his eyes were. I mean, I had crushes on boys before, but Chico was different. He gave me a feeling on the inside. The feeling wasn't sexual, but more like our energy was drawn to each other. Nikki and I continued to walk, and I felt in my back pocket for his phone number, and all I felt was lint. I immediately panicked. I checked all my pockets, but the paper was gone.

"I lost the freaking number. How will I reach him now?" I asked Nikki in a frustrated tone.

"Did you give him your number?" she asked.

"No," I lowered my head.

"Don't worry. I run into Chico's brother Nick all the time. I'll make sure he gets your number."

I believed her, but I wasn't confident I would see him again, which made me sad. I would often daydream about Chico. I would pretend he was my boyfriend, and he was in love with me, but then I would remember how stupid I was to lose the number and probably would never see him again.

My mother and I started staying home more often. We soon realized Frederick Ave was not as quiet as we thought. It was much calmer than the projects, but stuff was still happening around there. All the neighborhood guys started hanging in our house. It was also a warm place for them to hang out instead of standing outside all day. The guys naturally gravitated toward us. Maybe they could feel the realness of who we were.

Some of the guys were strict and stayed on my case. Some of them would let me smoke weed and do whatever I wanted. One guy named Morris was so cute, but he was a little older than me. Morris had the darkest features I had ever seen. His thick eyebrows were dark black, and out of control, his nose was long but perfectly shaped, and his lips were an off-pink color from smoking blunts. His looks were adorable.

Morris and I became extremely close. He was my big brother, but I secretly crushed on him a little. It was weird. I was attracted to him, but we had a sibling relationship. I loved him. He lived with his grandmother, whom he adored. He was in our house more than the other guys. He would lay across my bed and take naps after being so stoned out from smoking weed. I would call him Mr. Polo because that was his favorite brand of clothes to wear. I can't recall a time I didn't see him wearing Ralph Lauren.

I would argue with the guys sometimes because I wanted them to get out. Meet my neighborhood brothers. We have Reds who was just rude and obnoxious but was kind-hearted deep down. He had freckles, red hair, and straight teeth. Reds' feet would stink so bad, and all the guys would clown him about those dogs. We had Trey; he was one of my favorites but didn't play. He would twist my arm until I almost cried if I was acting too grown. Gus was quiet and calm. Gus and Trey were cousins, and if you saw one of them, the other wouldn't be far behind. Rell was light-skinned with dreads and had two golds on his side teeth. Rell loved smiling, and it fit his cute face. Gee was dark and handsome with a mellow personality.

Gee and Rell were close, and they both were women whores. Los was thick, with caramel skin and a cute chubby face. Rell and Los were best friends. Los was the first guy to come into our house, and he and my mother were close. Los was the first person we met around Frederick Ave, and he schooled us on where everything was in the neighborhood. Then there was Monk, who was dark, short, and stocky. Monk was the cheapest and sneakiest of them all. I mean, he was tight like a fish's pussy. Monk stayed at our house a lot as well. All the guys were adults except Morris and Reds. They all became my big brothers.

I was up one night sitting on the balcony when I saw this guy wearing all black. He walked slowly but steadily. I looked around my surroundings and then back to the guy. He looked at me with a hard-facial expression. Out of awkwardness, I smiled at him. He frowned. I felt stuck. I knew I could leave the balcony by just sliding the screen door open, but I was scared to move. He stared more intensely, without blinking. I wondered, *can he smell my fear*? I turned away from his eye contact. I pretended to sing a song with the hopes of when I looked back; he would be gone.

When I turned back, he was still there. He was now watching me with the stare of an owl. His eyes weren't blinking. Out of fear, I stood up to make my way back into the house. He slowly shook his head no and moved his hand towards the top of his jeans, where his pistol waited. I sat my ass back down and began to sweat and panic. I thought of calling my mother, but she wouldn't hear me through the patio door, nor did I want to alarm her. I would have preferred to get hurt alone than to involve my mother. I remained quiet.

"You Sunni, right?" he asked moving closer.

"Yes, I'm Sunni," I finally answered. I didn't respond right away. I was scared to admit I was Sunni. *I don't know why I was scared. It's not like I was in a gang or anything. Why* would some thug be after little ole me? So, what the fuck does he want? I'm sick of his ass!

"Nice to meet you," he said with a sarcastic grin.

"What do you want?" I boldly asked.

"I want the bread!" he demanded. He smirked with an evil look on his face.

"From who? No one in here has any money," I quickly responded.

"Remember my face. I'll be back to collect. Send the word to your brothers."

He slowly walked away. I ran to tell my mother and Morris. They both ran to the balcony, and the guy was nowhere in sight. He freaked me out. Morris was pissed, and he called all the guys over to discuss the threat. I kept replaying his words in my mind, especially the part about him coming back.

CHAPTER 10

NEW AREA SAME BS

I started Rock Glen Middle, also known as West Baltimore Middle School. I didn't know anyone there except Nikki, and she was in a different grade. This was the same school my cousin Diamond went to, but she had moved on to Western High School by now. Each grade at Rock Glen had a separate building, but they all connected in the middle. My classes were located in the 6th- grade building. The hallways were long and shallow.

A boy named Mike instantly liked me from the very first day of school. He wasn't my type at all. He had super big lips and bad acne. I was naturally friendly to people who liked me because I didn't receive pleasure from hurting people's feelings. I told him in a pleasant way that I wasn't interested. He didn't get it, or he just didn't care. He followed me around constantly. He tried to carry my books to every class. Thankfully, I only had two classes with him. On this particular day, I was irritated, and Mike was being extremely annoying. I was at my locker when he walked up.

"There goes my baby," he said in his so-called sexy voice.

I instantly rolled my eyes, shut the locker, and took a deep breath. "Mike, I told you before I'm not your baby."

"But you are my baby, and we go together. That's why I do everything for you," he said in a weak voice.

"Mike, not today!" I said as I walked towards my next class.

"Baby! You are my girl," he pleaded.

"We don't go together! LEAVE ME THE FUCK ALONE, DAMN!" I screamed.

The moment the words left my mouth, I instantly felt regret. I didn't quite understand how I lost control of my thoughts that fast, but I did. I yelled so loud it was as if there was an echo in the hall. Everyone turned and looked at us with frowned-up facial expressions, especially the girls. The hallways were filled with whispers and chatter.

"Damn, she didn't have to talk to him like that," one short girl stated with her nostrils flared.

"Don't worry about her, Mike, fuck her," a taller girl yelled.

"Fuck you, and you can take his annoying ass to follow you around," I responded, looking straight into her eyes.

She pretended as if she was coming towards me to fight. I dropped my books and thought, *here we go, here comes the unnecessary bullshit!*

"She's not even worth it," the tall girlfriend yelled. Her friend grabbed her arm before she reached me, and they walked the opposite way.

"I'm sorry, Sunni, I just really liked you," Mike said softly. He played right into the sympathy role by looking sad and pathetic.

I almost slapped his whining punk ass. He started all that drama; now, he wanted to play the victim. I told his weak ass I wasn't interested on the first day of school. The "Mike Issue" was the start of many people not liking me at the new school.

I came off like a completely cruel bitch to an innocent unattractive sweet guy who just had a crush on me. That was so not the case. I was anything but cruel. I was patient and nice to his annoying ass, but he caught me on the wrong day, at the wrong time. People will think and believe what they want, anyway. I learned many life lessons from Perkins, one being to never stress about other people's thoughts. Most of the negative things people dislike are the things they see in themselves. If they didn't like me, that was their issue, in their mind. Not my problem! Not my issue!

I grabbed my books off the floor and turned the corner to go to my next class. That's when I saw him. He was standing against a locker in the 7th-grade hallway. The bell rang, and I barely noticed. I stood there watching his demeanor. I watched how he talked, laughed, and goofed around with the other boys. I snapped out of my daydream and slowly walked to class.

I entered the classroom about two minutes late, and everyone looked up. A few of the girls rolled their eyes as if I was interrupting their class. The irony of females. They are always fucking angry. So, let me get this right, these chicks are upset because I yelled at Mike earlier, which has nothing to do with them, yet it gives them a reason to hate. For the life of me, I could not understand why females wasted so much energy on hating. I smiled at them.

"My apologies for being late," I humbly said to the teacher. I completely ignored the angry females. I couldn't concentrate on the schoolwork for the entire class. All I could think about was him. My teacher was incompetent. Her name was Mrs. Lorelox. Her favorite words were "Uhm," "one-second guys," and "let me think on that." When I asked her a question, her answer was always, "I don't know, but I will find out." I would often think, lady, what do you know? It was easy to lose focus in this history class anyway, but on this day, I was so in la-la land, I didn't hear a word she said. Once the class was over, I realized I would at least need notes to do my homework.

"Can I hold your notes, please?" I asked Brittany. She was the smart girl in the class that many people didn't talk to, but I liked her.

"Girl, you were in the same class. Where are your notes?" she asked.

"Please," I begged with an innocent smile.

"I want my notes back by lunchtime," she shoved them to my chest but not aggressively.

"Okay, chill. You will get them back. Girl, relax," I said to Brittany. I whispered under my breath, *damn, that girl needs to loosen up.*

When school let out, I decided to get on the bus instead of walking down Frederick Ave. It was fun walking home instead of getting on the rowdy bus for only two stops. The bus also took forever to pull off, and I was not particularly eager to sit there waiting to leave. So, I walked home on most days. One of the main reasons I enjoyed walking home was so I could walk past the woods. I've always loved nature. Something about the fresh air, the trees, the smell, and the birds chirping constantly reminded me that I was alive. I was sincerely grateful for life.

It was a cold, blistering day, and I didn't feel like walking, so I hopped on the bus with the hopes of getting warm. I didn't talk to anyone on the bus. I was listening to TLC album, "Crazy Sexy Cool," on my portable CD player. I felt a soft index finger swipe across my neck. I turned around, and everyone was looking the other way which instantly annoyed me.

"Who touched my neck?" I asked the crowd at the back of the bus.

"Girl ain't nobody touch you!" a boy yelled.

I rolled my eyes and turned back around and mumbled witty remarks under my breath. Someone slowly swiped their finger against my neck again. I removed my earphones from my ears. I frowned my face before I turned around. I had every intention to curse someone out, but before I could start my rant…

"I touched your neck," Chico said as he popped up from behind the chair.

"Boy, you better stop playing!" I responded before actually realizing it was Chico. My heart dropped. I knew I saw him earlier at the locker. A whole summer had passed since we first met at the house party. I couldn't believe he was right there in front of me. It was MY Chico.

"You thought I didn't see you earlier?" he asked with a suspicious look on his face.

"Earlier? When you were at the lockers?" I asked as if I didn't know what he was talking about. I was so embarrassed. I had no clue he saw me stalking him.

"Yes, I saw you looking at me, but you didn't even speak."

"Anty, who is that?" a pretty brown-skinned girl asked. She had big boobs and shapely hips.

I thought, *oh God is this his shapely cute brown girlfriend? Is she my competition? I can't compete with those boobs and hips. Shit, I only have nipples.* I looked down at my flat chest and then looked up at her big breasts, and I got a little upset on the inside. Just the thought of him being already spoken for made me sad. On top of that, this chick was out of my body's league. My face was attractive, soft, and noticeable. My body was slim and unnoticeable. I had a lot of nothing! No boobs, no ass, and no stomach. Well, let me be fair, I had a little bit of ass to fit my slim shape. I wasn't like a stick, straight up and down. I had a Black girl shape but with no weight to back it up.

I usually never compared myself to other girls, but I always noticed them. I admired what they had. The Westside chicks were curvy. I often joked with my friends and said their moms fed them a different kind of Similac milk.

"She's my new girlfriend," Chico finally responded to the busty girl as he looked in my direction.

"Oh, she's pretty, Anty," the girl responded as she looked me up and down.

"Thanks," I said with a fake smile. I blushed and thought, *did he just say I was his girlfriend?* I wanted to inquire about who the chick was. I gave Chico a look so he could explain who she was.

"This is my cousin Shawny," he said without hesitation.

"Your cousin?" I sighed with relief. I now knew she wasn't a threat. I thought to myself, *whoa, she is just a cousin, the Bitch is no threat to me, I can breathe now, OMG he said I was his girlfriend. I jumped out of my thoughts.*

"Yup, my cousin," he smiled at the thought of me being jealous.

"Why do you keep calling him Anty?" I asked Shawny.

"Cause he's my Anty! It's a family nickname that comes from his middle name," she replied. She pinched his cheeks, and he brushed her off.

"Call me boyfriend, oops, I meant Anty!" I said to Chico in a marking way. I hurried up and wrote my number down because my bus stop was coming up, and no way would I forget to give him my number this time. I gave him the number.

"Thanks for the number, since you never called me," Chico pointed out.

"I actually lost..." I started to explain, but the bus door opened, and the wind smacked my face. I leaned my foot over to step out when Chico grabbed me back.

"You are coming with us," Chico said while holding my waist.

"Boy, let me off this bus!" I yelled.

"I missed you all summer Sunni," he softly whispered in my ear. He stood behind me and put his arm around my neck.

"For real?" I asked while blushing. I stopped pretending I was getting off the bus. I just enjoyed his arms around my neck.

"If you are Anty's girlfriend, then you are my friend too now," Shawny said with authority.

The bus driver quickly shut the door and pulled off. A burst of air chilled the bus, and Chico's hot arm around my neck was comforting. I was stuck on the bus going up Beechfield with Chico and Shawny. I thought, *he missed me? He said I was his girlfriend. I can't believe I'm on this bus with Chico. I dreamed of this day, and now it's happening.* We laughed and played as we rode up the hill. I hadn't been past Frederick Avenue, so I was observing the neighborhood. I was also trying to remember how to get back home. A group of us ran off the bus before it barely stopped.

Shawny wasn't like any other girl I'd ever met before. She had so much personality. She was silly and fun. I mean, you never knew what would come out of her mouth. She would randomly make cat sounds for no reason. Real cat sounds! The girl was hilarious, which made me instantly like her. We quickly became a threesome. Shawny had an older sister named Tori, and Chico had an older brother named Nick. Chico and Nick looked like twins, and weirdly enough, Shawny and Tori looked just alike as well. They all lived together. I could sometimes spend the night with Chico because Shawny and I were friends. So, when I stayed over with Shawny, I got to be with Chico too.

Fortunately for our parents, we were innocent. Chico would lay his head on my lap for me to play in his hair. He was super affectionate. His touches were soft and gentle, and I loved the way he touched me. We were both virgins and in no rush to try sex, but we kissed a lot. I mean a lot of kissing. Nick would call us spitty mouths. We would sometimes argue just to make up and kiss. I would be in the middle of a sentence, and he would come behind me only to kiss my neck with his hot breath and soft lips. It made me blush every time he did it. Every so often, Chico would softly rub his finger across my neck. He did that to remind me of that day on the bus. I would randomly kiss Shawny too. I loved to squeeze her boobs and smack her butt. Not in a sexual way, but more in a fun way.

"Y'all are weird and gay. Yuck!" Tori yelled.

We laughed, and Shawny ran up to Tori and started trying to rub her down, smack her butt and kiss her.

"Come here, Sister. Come get some of these lips," Shawny teased.

"Shawny, I'm not playing with you. You better go ahead with that gay stuff," Tori yelled as she pushed Shawny away.

The more annoyed Tori would get, the funnier it would be. Wrestling and fighting were our ways of having fun. Nick was rough and had no sympathy for the fact we were girls, but Chico would take it easy on us. Nick would slam us, jump on us with his elbows or try to beat us to death with pillows. Shawny's sister Tori would jump in and help us.

Tori had the cutest little son named Mookie. Shawny and I argued over Mookie. Shawny was crazy. It was her nephew, but he would reach for me sometimes instead of her. She would catch an attitude and say, "Well, if he loves you more, then I don't care." I paid her no mind and picked up Mookie anyway. I loved kissing his cute little face.

Shawny would stop talking to me for the rest of the day. I'd laugh to myself and think, *this girl is nuts.* I soon realized Shawny was sensitive, which made me love her more because I was sensitive too. So, I understood her extreme level of drama. Chico's mother was gorgeous. Her name was Ms. Pear. She worked a lot, and she didn't play about her sons. I saw why her sons were so handsome. She had that same pretty brown milky skin and lovely hair that her sons inherited. Shawny and I loved to watch Ms. Pear's butt when she walked away. Shawny would whisper, "Damn Aunt Pear phat to death… Meowwwwww!" (her famous cat sound)

Late one evening, Chico was walking me home. We were holding hands, looking corny, I'm sure. We stopped at Beechfield Rec Center and talked to Coach L. The recreation center at Beechfield was our hangout spot. I watched Chico play a little basketball with his boys. Every so often, he would look at me and smile. I'd think, *damn, he is gorgeous. I can't believe he's mine. I love him so much.* I know this was considered to be puppy love, but nope this was dog love. I just didn't know it at the time.

My mom was down Perkins celebrating her birthday, so I was in no rush to get home. Chico and I planned to go into my room alone and kiss or, in my mind, maybe even take it to the next step. We never really talked about sex. I was more curious about it than he was. He said we didn't have to be like everyone else; when we were ready, we would know.

I didn't want to hear that shit! I thought I was ready, but Chico would always remind me how crazy people act once they start having sex. We didn't want crazy; our bond was perfect with no extra complications. It got dark, so we left the rec. We crossed the street to my apartment complex. Just as we crossed the street, we heard gunshots. He grabbed me, and we hid on the side of the building.

"Okay, this is as far as I'm walking you," he said with a severe but frightful face.

"What? You better walk me home," I responded with an attitude.

"Let's sit here for ten minutes after the shooting stops," he suggested.

"The shots stopped. Let's go!" I demanded.

We were both scared, but he was more afraid. I looked at Chico's face, and I saw he wasn't playing. He would really leave me. He noticed how I looked at him with my eyebrows frowned and my lips curled. Sometimes it was hard for me to understand other people's fears and doubts. The sad truth is I had seen too much at a young age, including a dead body, and it became normal to expect bad things to happen. When I looked into Chico's eyes, I realized his fear of not wanting to move was very normal. It showed me he had an ordinary childhood and bad things rarely happened to him. For a split second, I envied him. I should've had that same fear in my eyes, but my childhood wasn't ordinary.

I was eager to make sure everyone was okay. In the back of my mind, I knew my mother was safe because she wasn't home, but I worried about the guys (my brothers). This was my first-time hearing gunshots in this area, so I knew it didn't happen often. We slowly walked past each apartment building. We saw a crowd. The crowd wasn't at my building; however, they were at the building next to mine. Knowing the group of people wasn't at my apartment gave me quick relief. It didn't last long. We saw Rell's shirt covered in blood, and he was banging on the brick wall.

"Fuck, fuck, fuck!" he screamed. He was crying, and his knuckles were bleeding.

I knew it had to be one of the guys. Sadly it was Los. I instantly felt grief. Los was the first guy we met around F & T.

He was the reason all the other guys hung out in our house. I cried in Chico's chest, and he hugged me tightly. Chico knew Los too, so he also felt the grief. He had a deep sadness in his eyes that showed remorse.

I called down Perkins and told my mother someone killed Los. The bad news devastated her. She told me she would be home right away. Although we didn't know Los for years, it felt like years. He was the only one who gave me money every morning for school. I shared many intimate long talks with him. His heart was pure and I knew I would miss his presence and his big smile. The next few weeks were a blur. Everything was quiet. Nothing was moving except the trees, which seemed to whistle louder.

The guys continued to come to our apartment, but there was no laughter, no jokes, no fun, only silence. Days quickly turned into weeks. One day I came home, and everyone was smoking weed quietly in the living room. My mother was sitting at the dining room table with Danny. Danny was our neighbor in the building next to us. Danny and my mother shared a horrible common interest. They both were amazing mothers with habits.

"Alright, this is enough!" I blurted out to everyone in the room.

"What do you mean, Lil Sis?" Rell asked.

"Los wouldn't want us sitting around with our heads hung low, depressed, quiet, and sad," I said in an inspiring tone.

"But this shit is just so fucked up!" Morris stated loudly.

"I know, but we have to stop avoiding what happened by being quiet and angry. Instead, let's talk about Los because I miss him," I pleaded.

"Talk about him for what? What the hell good will that do? HE'S GONE!" Morris replied with emotion.

"Yeah, it really ain't shit to talk about. He's gone," Rell added.

"Do you trust me?" I asked with a look of concern.

"Of course, but what does that have to do with anything?" Morris answered first.

"I'm younger than all of you, and these sad vibes are wearing me down. Do you want to send me into a deep depression? I want to talk about Los."

"FINE TALK!" Rell screamed.

I talked about all the fun times I had with Los and how he opened up to us when we first moved to Frederick Ave. I spoke of his silly moments, like the day he missed the bottom step and fell but got up quickly.

"Did anybody see that?" Los asked.

"I DID!" I laughed. I kept laughing to the point Los had no choice but to laugh with me.

"Girl, your ass is silly. Morris better stop smoking that weed with you," he stated.

I joked with him that entire day, calling him "Sonic the Hedgehog" since he got up so fast. Yeah, that was a good day with Los. As I continued to reminisce on all my memorable encounters with Los, the guys joined in. They started telling their own crazy stories about Los. They expressed how they missed him and how they were angry that he was murdered outside alone. They expressed how if they would have been there, things could've gone differently. They smoked and drank lots of liquor. We continued to talk about Los for hours. We laughed, cried, and even got angry, but we did it together. The six of us created a bond that night that was unforgettable.

I learned something special that day. I learned men didn't know how to handle pain or emotions. It's the reason women endure childbirth, menstrual cycles, hormones, and whatever other mental stress that a man couldn't handle. They didn't know what to do with the pain or how to deal with the emotions. They used anger as their first emotion. I also sympathized with men because I knew sometimes they just wanted to be vulnerable and let go of their macho man image. I couldn't help, but wonder *did the guy in all black killed Los? He did say he would be back. He made a point to tell me he would come to collect. Did he come to collect from Los? Should I be worried? I never saw him again, and that was months ago. Plus, if it were him, the guys would know. No, I'm good—no need to worry about him.*

CHAPTER 11

MY TINK

Chico and Shawny started coming to my place more often. After school, we would go to my house to eat. We kept a lot of food because I was my mother's only child, so snacks stayed in our cabinets longer than most families. Shawny loved to eat. She even had a food dance that she would do whenever food was around. Soon as she would come in, she would go straight to the refrigerator. I would laugh uncontrollably when she found what food she liked and started doing her food dance.

I didn't go to Shawny and Chico's house as much as I did at first because I started enjoying being home. I still went to their house but not daily. I met another friend in my complex named May. She was cool, and we hung out a lot. My mother would let Chico and I sit in the living room and watch a movie or listen to music because she trusted us.

Chico gave me a kitten from his cat's litter. I named him Tink. Not only was he my first real pet, but he came from Chico, which made me love him more. Tink and I were very close. I was an only child, so I enjoyed Tink's body heat sleeping with me, and having a pet that depended on me. I looked forward to seeing him whenever I entered our home.

Tink had somehow gotten out of the house, which was strange because he was comfortable being a "house cat," but he had an itch every so often to get some air. I was devastated he got out. Everyone told me that animals always find their way back home. May and I went looking and screaming "Tink!" around the entire neighborhood. She helped me look for Tink every day for a week.

It had been two weeks, and Tink still didn't come back, nor could I find him. I was so worried. My mother told me cats were independent, and they could survive, but he loved me, and he would surely be back. I told Chico Tink was gone, and he comforted me, but I think he was tired of hearing about Tink. I finally stopped whining about it and prayed that Tink found safe shelter and would return after he finished his little cat ventures.

The softness I had for my cat was a small reminder that confirmed I was still a sweet, sensitive child. No matter what life threw at me, I was still a minor, and my heart was pure. I had to tell myself this when I found myself being overly sensitive. It made me happy to know I still had a heart, and I could still feel so much emotion, even for a cat. I've lost people that I deeply cared for; however, I cared about this cat too. Why? I never even liked cats. I always thought they were sneaky and suspicious. I realized it wasn't where you got love from; it was the genuine love that caused an attachment. My cat loved me, and I accepted all love. That's the pleasure of being a child.

Chico and I went to the store to get some crab sticks and french fries. It was dark outside, and Chico needed to get home soon, so we tried to hurry up. I ran across the street in the intersection, barely missing a car that was speeding by. A guy beeped his horn and yelled profanity from his window. I put up my middle finger. I walked into the Chinese carryout in a rush.

"Mama! Can you drop me some crab sticks fried hard and a dollar fry?" I yelled.

"Okay, Sunni!" The Chinese woman responded.

"Did you see me in the line waiting to order?" a thick girl in the store rudely asked.

"Yes, I saw you, but you standing there waiting to order is not my problem, baby. You can surely order now," I sarcastically smiled.

"Little girl, you are about to get yourself smacked!" she replied in a furious tone.

I just smiled at her. That's what I do. I just smile. Anyone who tells me what they are ABOUT to do is NOT ABOUT to do shit. I've been in enough fights to know these fake tough shit-talkers. They are always ABOUT to do something. I usually just smile and look around to see what I can hit them with if they decide to actually do something. Honestly, I just wanted my food so Chico and I could eat before he had to leave. We walked outside to wait.

"Sunni, your mouth is so slick. You did cut the line," Chico said in a low tone as he grabbed my arm to pull me to the side.

"FUCK HER! I didn't cut the line; I just yelled my order out. It's not my fault she is standing there like a mute," I yelled loud enough for her to hear me.

"See, that's what I'm talking about, Sunni. Your slick mouth. You're too pretty to be acting like that. You don't always have to respond," his tone was annoyed.

Is he taking that bitch side? I thought. No, he's not. He's being reasonable. He's being Chico, and I'm showing my ass. Chico despised conflict. I could have asked her did she already order before I came into the store yelling, but I didn't. I did what I wanted to do at the moment. It wasn't my responsibility to make sure she ordered. I looked at Chico and smiled. I walked over to him and kissed him.

"That's why I love you, Chico. You balance me out. I need you to check me when I'm wrong. I'll watch my mouth, okay," I spoke in a low, seductive voice.

"I love you too, Sunni," he kissed me back.

"I'm hungry. We didn't eat since this morning," I said as my stomach growled.

"I'm hungry too. Are you going to apologize?" he asked.

"FUCK NO, STILL FUCK HER!" I yelled.

"Wow!" Chico just laughed and shook his head. That fast our little fight was over, and that's usually how quickly our fights ended. I walked back into the store.

"Order ready, Sunni," the Chinese woman yelled.

"Thanks, Mama!" I walked past the girl, got my order, and walked back towards the door.

"Bitch!" the thick girl mumbled under her breath.

"Come on!" Chico grabbed my arm.

"See, all of that because I yelled out my order, and you wanted me to apologize to that scavenger?" I quickly responded to Chico.

I walked away with Chico; I didn't respond to her calling me a Bitch. I was over it. I devoured my first french fry and moved on. I thought nothing of it. I got my food, and she was still there waiting, so why would I be mad. That was my personality. I say and do whatever I want, and then I'm over it.

I never put too much energy into any situation, especially not a female. Her calling me a bitch was funny now. I threw another french fry in my mouth and walked to the curb. We walked across the street, and we saw Tink. There he was on the road, dead, lifeless, with no energy, no movement, no love, just dead. I immediately started crying. He almost made it home. He got hit by a car right by our house. My friend May came and hugged me.

"I didn't want you to see Tink like that. I was trying to catch you before you came across the street. He just got hit," My friend May said.

"I wish I didn't see him like that. He looks afraid," I replied.

Tink's mouth was pushed so far back you could see his entire jawline. His face looked deformed, and the look in his eyes was fear. I cried in Chico's chest, and May held my hand. I thought, *oh no, not my Tink*. He wasn't just a cat to me; he was my friend, and up until I got him, I didn't even like cats. I was angry with God again. I asked God, "Why couldn't you just keep Tink away? Why did you make me see death again? If you had to take Tink, why did he have to die by the house?" Now I felt like shit. I would have much preferred to think that Tink just ran away. Soon as I walked into the house, my mother knew something was wrong.

"What's wrong?" my mother asked.

"Tink is dead; he got hit by a car," I said coldly before I burst into tears.

"Oh no, baby. I'm sorry Sunni," my mother cried too. She loved Tink as well. I went into my room and shut my door, and cried until I fell asleep.

The next day, I gathered all of Tink's toys along with his bed that he never slept in, and put it all in a box. I took a hot shower and told myself, *Okay, Sunni, let this go now. You must be strong!* That's what I did, and I let it go. I took all Tink's stuff to the dumpster and cried my last cry, and told him I loved him. I tried to block the image out of my mind like I had to do the day I saw Toni's dead body on the cold concrete. Goodbye Tink. I turned to walk away from the dumpster with my head down and bumped into someone. I looked up, and it was Mr.

ALL BLACK. The guy who scared me on the balcony was back, and here I was all alone. *FUCK!*

"What the fuck do you want!?" I yelled as loud as I could. I prayed someone could hear my big mouth and come save me.

"I told you I would be back," he said in a low vicious tone.

I prayed again that someone heard my yell. Even in a moment of fear, I noticed how handsome he was. He had dark smooth skin with long eyelashes and straight teeth. *Why am I noticing his looks before he blows my brains out? What the hell is wrong with me? What does he want? Did he kill Los, and now he coming for me? No, that's stupid. Why would he come for me?* He pulled me out of my deep thought.

"Did you hear me?" he loudly asked.

"No," I quickly responded. I did not hear him. Not one word.

"Remember my face Sunni, I'll be back to collect," he then slowly walked away.

CHAPTER 12

A DOLL WITH SOME HONEY

I missed Honey. We lost contact when I moved from my Aunt Shelby's house. I found her mother's number in my mom's little black book. I called the number and asked if I could speak to Honey. Liz, Honey's mother, answered and informed me Honey had moved out, and she now had two kids. I knew about her first child Seth. I met him before I left Perkins, and I couldn't believe he belonged to Honey. Liz and I talked for about an hour before I finally hung up and called Honey. I told Honey that mommy and I missed her.

Honey's children's father was abusive. His name was Big Seth. She was finally getting away from his mental and physical abuse. I told her to come over to our house, and I had someone I think she would be interested in dating. Honey came over the following weekend. I hooked her up with Rell. I don't know why I hooked her up with Rell, especially since I knew he was a women whore. He would often bring the little sluts to our house. I guess I thought of him because he was a good person and very giving. I knew he wouldn't abuse Honey or harm her. I never thought it would go further than casual fun. I figured he could help her get her mind off Big Seth.

Honey came to our house the following weekend. Soon as I opened the door, I jumped on her and kissed her everywhere. I kissed her lips, her nose, her forehead, and her chubby cheeks. Oh, how I missed my Honey. She missed me too. She laughed and giggled.

"Girl, your little ass is still crazy," Honey said.

"You better know it," I replied.

We talked for hours about every little detail we had missed from each other's lives. I told Honey all about Chico and how much I loved him. Later that night, she met Rell. They seemed to have an instant sexual attraction. Our house became live on the weekends, so all the guys were over. Morris and I sat at the dining room table eating a cheesesteak that he had bought me. He always made sure I was good, and by now, Morris loved my mother too. He cared for her like he would love his own mother, but he wanted her to get herself together. They argued a lot because he held her accountable. He could see the beautiful person she was, and he wanted the best for us. That made me love Morris more because he cared. Our house wasn't just a hangout spot to him. We became his family.

Honey walked over to me with speed. "Give me a bite," Honey demanded.

"You better ask Rell to feed you," I said in a joking way. She completely ignored me and picked up my sub, and took a big sloppy bite.

"Damn, her ass is greedy! Where did you get her from?" Morris asked in a joking tone.

"Boy, I been in the picture," Honey replied to Morris.

"I don't like greedy people. Especially the kind that just walks around begging and shit," Morris said.

"Y'all crazy!" I joined in.

"Greedy? Your long-head ass needs to shut up with those tight pants. Your pants so tight I can count your change," Honey Joked.

"Got damn, your one titty is so long it gets sucked by your navel," Morris responded.

This was the beginning of Honey's and Morris's crack on each other relationship. They clowned each other from the first day they met. The jokes were foolish and corny, but I loved the entertainment. Sometimes the corniest jokes were the funniest, especially when you're high. After I smoked weed, those two would be hilarious. I wasn't an official pothead. I would randomly sneak and smoke. I never smoked in front of my mother, but she caught me stoned a few times.

"Why did you hook me up with Rell? I mean, he's sexy, but he's a red bone. Gee is more my type," Honey exclaimed.

"Why, Gee?" I asked.

"Cause he dark and handsome. That's my kind of guy."

"Well, this is your first meet-up. Go for Gee if you like him more. You are a single free woman! I'm done playing Cupid," I said as I hunched my shoulders.

"I was already talking to Rell on the phone," she said. She went back and sat with Rell and played in his hair when unexpectedly, a dread fell out in her hand. She had the most awkward look on her face. Honey was so silly. She looked at me with a goofy facial expression showing me the dread in her hand. I laughed so hard.

"Oh shit, what should I do with it?" her lips moved without sound.

"Hide it," I whispered.

She slid the dread in her bra. That made me laugh harder. I thought, *did this girl just put his dread in her bra?* I could not stop laughing. Rell wasn't aware one of his dreads fell out of his head. He was drunk and extra talkative. We had so much fun that night. As the night slowed down, Rell and Honey crept off, had sex, and crashed on the couch. Some people fell asleep right on the floor. Morris and I slept in my bed together. I had two twin beds pushed together like one King-sized bed. So, he would be on one twin bed, and I would be on the other. My bedroom door was always open. He was always fully dressed and never got under the covers. He would just be too drunk to go home. Morris tried to hang with the older guys, but he wasn't a drinker. We were close, but he never crossed the line.

I had an open relationship with Morris, and I could tell him anything, even about Chico and me. When the house would quiet down, and we'd be alone, we talked for hours. He'd tell me about his grandmother and the issues he had with his mother. He told me that's why he was always so hard on my mother because he wanted her to do better with me.

These talks Morris and I had were always intimate and profound. He wasn't critical or judgmental but would give me firm advice when I needed it. I loved Morris a lot, not the way I loved Chico but, I wanted him in my life forever. I often felt like we only moved to Frederick Ave to meet these special guys. They all impacted my life in one way or another. They were my brothers.

Monk was dating a bad girl named Doll. She had pretty brown skin with big full lips and straight teeth. Her eyes were almond-shaped, and she had cute brown freckles around her little nose. She wore her hair in Pixie braids that she had professionally done by the African braiders. Doll was attractive and for sure out of Monk's League. We would say behind his back, *how did he get her?* She stayed at our house during the week with Monk. We became close, and Honey became jealous. I would expect nothing less from Honey. She never wanted to share me with anyone. What she didn't know is that no one could ever take her place. Doll had her place in my heart that didn't threaten my relationship with Honey.

I learned a lot from Doll. There were two things she didn't play about, men and money. You must pay to play. She was calm but aggressive. I admired her go-getter style. She wasn't a gold digger, but she was a young woman who needed things, and she would get her necessities by any means. Why go without? Or why lay on your back and be broke? I was young and a virgin, so I wasn't lying on my back, side, or stomach, but I watched how Doll moved, and I took mental notes.

I told myself I would never have sex and be broke. Monk was cheap, and Doll was not having it. She took whatever money she wanted right out of his pocket. It killed him on the inside. I could see it all over his face. Doll gave me some of his money too. "I'm about to spend your money, cheap ass," I teased Monk. He was so annoyed with me, but he knew Doll was the boss.

One early evening Honey and I were in the kitchen when we heard screaming from the living room. We looked at each other simultaneously. We both left the kitchen at the same time to see what was going on. We were not prepared for what we saw. Doll was beating Monk up like he stole something. Left hook, right hook, double left hook, and right hook again!

"Doll, stop! You going to make me fuck you up! Stop!" Monk screamed."

"Stop! Oh, you want me to stop, huh? Did you take the time to stop talking to that Bitch?" Doll responded as she punched Monk nonstop.

"Y'all better get her!" Monk screamed. He looked at us to defuse the situation. I turned my head.

I thought to myself, *I know when to mind my business, and this was one of those times.* Doll was a beast with fighting. I wondered, *how could someone so pretty and feminine be so tough too?* Weirdly enough, I admired her more. Not only was she attractive, but she didn't take any crap. Apparently, Monk was talking to some chick on the phone, and Doll found out. He lied about it, which made Doll angrier. Men can be so stupid; they have no idea how to be discreet. We clowned Monk for weeks because he pretty much got beat up by a girl. Well, at least it was his girl.

Doll took an interest in my appearance. She did my hair and bought me little outfits. Doll's passion was hair, and I loved being her student. Doing hair was her gift. Until this point, I didn't care much about how I looked. I took no extra effort to enhance my beauty. I would brush my teeth because I always had a thing for white teeth. I would make sure my hair was neat and my clothes matched, but that was about it.

People always said I was pretty, but I never thought to take the extra time to look better. I had a nice length of hair, decent features, long lashes, and white teeth. I was confident with what I saw in the mirror. I wasn't self-absorbed, nor did I want to spend hours looking cute for others. I liked to wash my ass, brush my teeth, throw on some clothes and start my day.

My appearance was the last thing on my mind, and having fun was the first thing I thought of when starting my day. Doll would say in a settled voice, "Sunni, you are pretty, but you are a plain Jane." So, she would spice me up a little. I still had my own style but learned to get out of the safe box. Money wasn't flowing abundantly for me to dress and alter my style the way I wanted to, so I had to work with the clothes I already had.

Honey was beautiful and kept herself looking great too, so I could have easily picked up these feminine habits from her, but I didn't. Honey also cared about my appearance ever since I was seven. She always cared. I think we naturally don't want to listen to our siblings. Although Honey wasn't my real sister, we grew up like real sisters. Honey's approach was different. Our conversation about how I looked went a little like this…

"Sunni, change that sweater and put this on," Honey would demand.

"Why? I like this sweater!" I questioned.

"Just do it, trust me!" End of conversation. I'd huff and puff but put on whatever she said.

Doll was a blunt soft-spoken diva! Doll and I conversation about appearance went a little like this…

"That's tacky boo, let me show you something," Doll would calmly say.

"Why is it tacky?" I questioned.

"It's not stylish, but it could be if you take off the shirt and tie this around your waist," she would explain.

I took more to the explanatory approach. I was a pre-teen, and overnight my appearance mattered. I started caring about my hair and taking the time to iron my clothes and look more presentable. I never wanted to be like Honey or Doll. I was always comfortable in my own skin. I wasn't an envious person, so if someone was gorgeous, I admired their beauty, but I didn't yearn to be them. I was surrounded with beauty before either of them came into my life. My mom's beauty was enough (inside and out).

I realized from these young ladies that every soul that enters your life is there for a reason. Doll appeared in my life to show me how to be a feminine young lady and how NOT to take it easy on men. Honey appeared in my life to be a part of my life long term. It was just that simple. Doll was doing my hair in the living room when Honey came into the house distraught. Honey came over every weekend, our place was fun, and it was always something to do.

"Oh my God, I have to tell y'all!" Honey stated with a worrisome look on her face.

"Oh Lord Honey," Doll snickered quietly.

"You look worried, Sis. What's wrong?" I asked as I laughed at Doll's facial expression.

"I'm pregnant, and it's Rell's baby," She blurted out.

"What! Did you tell him?" I asked.

"No, I'm scared. We only slept with each other one time," Honey responded. She looked away as if she was in deep thought.

This was some juicy news, not the regular ordinary news. I instantly felt scared for Honey. Rell could've been excited about having a baby because this would be his first child, or it could've upset him because he hardly knew Honey. Honey told Rell later that night, and they argued. They later decided to date throughout her pregnancy. I would soon be an aunt again.

Morris and I stood in front of my apartment building talking about this new girl he was seeing and how she was acting pressed. I walked close to him, and he just looked at me. I took my index finger and lightly wiped his eyebrows. They were thick and out of control. The hairs on his eyebrows would be all over the place, and it drove me insane. I was so close to his face that our lips could've touched, and they almost did. After I fixed his eyebrows, I walked back and stood in my spot.

Morris continued to talk about the girl. We had a weird relationship. I fixed his eyebrows, touched his hair, popped his collar, or whatever needed to be done. He would buckle my belt on my pants without asking or throw a hat at me when I was on my way out the door in the blistering winter. We didn't ask, we just did. I never looked at it like flirting. It was just our bond. The girl he was talking about was so thirsty. She unexpectedly walked upon us.

"Well, hello. Didn't you get my page? What your beeper not working or something?" the thirsty chick quizzed.

"Chill, I was going to hit you back. I was tied up," Morris said in a blunt tone.

"Really? Tied up with who? Her?" she asked. She looked at me with her nose frowned up.

"See you later, Boo," I interrupted. I looked Morris dead in his eyes and gave him a sexy smile. I walked off, grinning to myself. I thought to myself, *Who does she think she is, coming over here getting smart? She got me fucked up.* I called him Boo to annoy her. I did it just to get under her skin. When I came from Chico's later that night, Morris came into my room and got in my face.

"Why do you like to start shit? I had to hear that chick mouth for like an hour about that "Boo shit," Morris growled.

"Why you mad, Boo?" I asked with laughter.

"You are not funny, Sunni," Morris replied firmly.

"Morris, get out of my face before I kiss you," I said as I moved closer to him, breathing right in his face.

He looked at me with an unusual look on his face. He didn't look confused or scared, but he had a look I never saw before. I couldn't read his thoughts, so out of nowhere, I kissed his lips. He kissed me back. He put his arm around me, and we savored the moment. My juices were flowing, but my mind was racing. I could tell his mind was racing too. At the same time, we decided just to enjoy the intense kiss. Our bodies loosely let go of the tension, and we kissed with passion. It was well overdue. It wasn't about Chico or Morris chicks; It was a moment that needed to happen, and that's all it was. Just a moment. After the kiss, we looked at each other with silence between us. Neither one of us moved. We froze in that moment.

"Sunni, we could never do this again," Morris said as he whispered with his lips still pressed against mine.

"I'm so sorry I crossed the line," I whispered back.

"Don't be sorry. It just happened. We both crossed the line, but we are too close to ever fuck up our friendship," Morris said.

"I agree," I responded.

We shook on, never crossing the line again. We agreed not to be awkward around each other. We didn't change our routine. We went back to normal. I continued to fix Morris's eyebrows, and he continued to make sure I was warm. Our late-night talks were the same, and we never spoke of the kiss. I felt guilty for kissing someone other than Chico. I loved Chico, but to be honest, I loved Morris too. He was my friend and so damn handsome. It was hard to separate the two feelings: friendship and lust. After the kiss, we knew our friendship was more important than lust. Chico was my true love, and Morris was my handsome-ass irresistible friend.

CHAPTER 13

NOTHING LASTS FOREVER

My curiosity about sex grew stronger and stronger. I always told my mother everything, even the most uncomfortable things. We were sitting on her bed in her room when I decided to bring up the sex topic.

"Ma, when I'm ready to have sex, what do I need to do?" I boldly asked my mother.

She almost spit her Pepsi on the floor. She slowly put her glass of soda on the nightstand. "Are you ready to have sex, Sunni?" she asked with her eyebrows raised.

"No, but I think about it," I quickly responded.

"That's normal. Come in the kitchen with me," my mother said as she walked over to her nightstand. She opened the drawer at her nightstand and grabbed something. I thought, *oh lord, what's about to happen?* We walked to the kitchen, and my mom picked up a banana.

"Picture this banana being a penis," my mother said while holding the banana in the air.

I giggled. My mom saying the word "penis" sounded so dirty. She then pulled out a condom and showed me how to put the condom on the banana. She took the condom out of the wrapper and roughly grabbed the banana. She slid it on with just her thumb and her index finger. The condom fitted snugly, and it was hardly any rubber left. Watching her put the condom on the big banana scared the shit out of me.

"Always make sure you protect yourself from STDs and pregnancy, now let me show you the process," she said with a faint smirk.

"The process? No thanks, ma, I don't need to see the process," I quickly responded with an anxious look on my face. Before I could finish the words out of my mouth, my mother took the banana and jammed it through a white powder donut with aggression. The powder donut was crumbling into pieces. There were small white crumbs all over the table.

"Now tell me when you ready to talk about birth control," she said in a sarcastic tone. She walked back to her room.

The banana and donut demonstration terrified me. I didn't want my little vagina to crumble up into pieces of white crumbs. My mom made her point, and just that fast, sex was out of my mind. I knew when I was ready; she would give me all the tools I needed. Our open relationship made me feel like I was in no rush to be an adult. Although I had been in some adult situations, I truly enjoyed being a child. There were no limits with me and my mother. We talked about men, dating, sex, drugs, vaginas, dicks, or anything we wanted to talk about at the moment. That's why this day would surely break her heart.

This was the day I told my mother about "The Devil." My mother never knew what happened to me at Sheila's house. I didn't comprehend what happened until I saw my first porn tape down Perkins, which I snuck and watched behind Honey's back. The day I first saw porn is when I realized the bone that perverted piece of shit had me licking was his penis. I didn't tell my mother right away because so much was going on down Perkins with the fast lifestyle we were both living. I tried to block out what happened, but it never truly left. I would often remember the encounter, and it made me want to vomit each time. For whatever reason, I told her on this day. Her heart broke into a million pieces. She cried hysterically and paced back and forth.

"Sunni, why didn't you tell me? You are my best friend. You know you can tell me anything. Why Sunni, why?" she asked as her voice crumbled.

"I'm sorry, Ma, I didn't understand what happened when I was four," I cried.

"I'm a kill that Bitch!" she screamed as tears streamed down her face.

We talked and cried for about an hour. I told my mother it wasn't her fault, and there was no way she could've known. I told her she did everything right as a mother. He was just a clever pervert, and he was smart enough to molest me in a way that wouldn't cause me pain. I gave her an entire breakdown of how it happened and how Little Kevin knew it happened. I told her Little Kevin tried to protect me but was too scared to tell on his brother. My mother started searching for her black phone book. She threw things all over the place in her room as she searched in frustration. She found the book and dialed Sheila's number so aggressively that I thought the buttons would break. After three rings, Sheila answered.

"Hello," Sheila answered with a pleasant phone voice.

"This is Queen," my mother said without saying hello back and avoiding all small talk.

"Hi Queen, how are you, baby? I haven't heard from you in years, how…" Sheila tried to ask in an eager tone.

My mother cut her off mid-sentence and got straight to the point. "Did you know what your son did to my daughter?" she asked with passion.

Sheila said nothing.

"You are dead to me, and when I find your son, you will be wearing a black dress," my mother barked.

Sheila got quiet, really quiet. She never asked what son? Or what happened? Or do what to your daughter? She just got quiet. Her silence spoke volumes, and it let us know she knew what happened. We assumed at some point, Little Kevin told his mother what Trayvon did.

My mother hung up the phone and immediately started looking for Trayvon. She pulled all her street contacts and put the word out that she was looking for him. She stayed on the phone for hours. This became her main focus for weeks to come. We eventually found out he was in jail for raping a pregnant woman and throwing her off a balcony. Unfortunately for him, jail was not a safe place to hide when karma was coming for him. Let's just say he encountered a bone or 2. A few weeks went by, and Morris, Rell, my mother, and I were in the house with the radio blasting.

"Did y'all hear that?" I screamed over the music.

"I think I heard something. Cut the music down!" Morris yelled.

"I knew I heard something," I said as I went to cut the music down. Rell walked towards the door, but before he reached the door, the door was kicked in.

The police were running into the house screaming, "EVERYONE GET ON THE FLOOR!"

We all got on the floor, on our stomachs. Morris and I lay side by side. My mother and Rell lay side by side, but they were across from Morris and me. There was fear in the room. I saw the fear in my mother's eyes, and it was disturbing. Rell had a guilty look on his face as if he had drugs on him, and Morris looked like he wasn't in the mood to be sitting down at Central Booking. I feared my life would change. That's all I feared at that moment.

"Is there anyone else in the house?" a cop asked with an annoying deep voice.

"No," my mother answered as she kept her head low to the floor, never looking up.

"Who's house is this?" he asked.

"Mines," my mother answered as she kept her head on the floor.

"Where is he?" another officer asked. He pulled out a picture and pointed to the face on the image.

No one answered. The cops started their search.

I looked my mother dead in her eyes and screamed, "NOT AGAIN MA, NOT AGAIN, I CAN'T DO THIS AGAIN!"

"I'm sorry, baby, I'm so sorry," my mother cried and, it was the first time she looked up from the floor.

The cop told both of us to shut up. At that very moment, I looked up at the cop. It was the first time I had looked up. I kept my eyes down on purpose to avoid the situation. I thought if I just looked away, they would go away. His voice was so familiar. It was him! He was the mysterious guy who tried to scare the hell out of me in all black.

He was the handsome guy that told me to remember his face at the dumpster. *Was he an undercover cop? What the fuck is going on, I thought?* They shoved the picture in Rell's face and asked him about Reds? Reds hadn't been in our house for months, but apparently, he had done something because they raided our home looking for him. I turned and looked at Morris in his eyes. For a moment, we just stared at each other, eye to eye.

The cops didn't scare me. At least this time, they talked to me like I was a child. I feared my mother and I would be split up again. I also wanted to tell Morris that the cop was the guy in all black that I had seen on the balcony that day, but what could Morris do? The mother fucker was a cop. I kept it to myself for the moment; it could do no good. It left me puzzled, though. Morris looked at me while I was in deep thought. He was waiting for me to say something.

"Morris, I'm so tired," I finally said.

"Sunni, it will be okay, just be quiet, Boo," Morris whispered. He noticed the fear in my eyes.

"Will it be okay?" I asked with sarcasm. I refused to look at my mother again because it was too painful, so I only looked at Morris.

"Get on your feet!" a cop said to Morris. Morris stood up.

"Where are you taking him? He didn't do anything!" I said.

"Sis, be quiet, please," Rell said with his index finger over his lips.

"Okay, dag, they don't own us. We can speak," I sarcastically said loud enough for the cops to hear me. I looked at Morris walk away with them and decided to be quiet. I heard them hitting Morris, so I stood up to help him.

"GET THE FUCK BACK ON THE FLOOR!" the dirty cop said.

"Why are you hitting him? He doesn't know anything!" I yelled.

"You better tell your little girlfriend to shut up!" the dirty cop told Morris as he landed another blow across his face.

Morris didn't have to tell me. I shut up and realized the cops were in control. It pained me to see them brutally punching Morris, and none of us could help him. Rell almost got up to defend Morris, but we all shook our heads no before he went to make a move. Every blow they punched to Morris's face hurt me in the pit of my stomach. Every moment I couldn't help him was torture. Morris remained quiet and took the beating like a man, but he wasn't a man. He was a teenager, and although he hung with an older crowd, he was still a minor. I loved Morris, and it took great discipline to stand by and do nothing.

Forty-five minutes later, they left. They arrested no one, nor did they have a warrant. They just wanted Reds, but they beat up Morris in the process. They also conveniently kept the money and drugs they confiscated. It didn't matter they were gone; the trauma was done. I was tired. My mother and I talked after they left.

I told her about the cop being the guy in all black. We could not figure out his intentions. It made us wonder, were they even cops? They were supposedly undercover or knocker cops. Is that why they didn't lock anyone up and didn't show a warrant. Maybe Morris knew but didn't want to tell us since they happily beat him up for no reason. Either way, the damage was done.

My mother suggested I live with my father so she could take the time to get herself together. I agreed. We cried and cried because we knew it would be hard to separate. My mother called my father and told him he needed to come and get me, and it was his turn to be the primary parent for a while. My father didn't ask any questions. He simply said, "I'm on my way."

I was terrified. I had never lived with my father or even been around him longer than a weekend. When I agreed to go live with my father, it didn't hit me right away that I'd have to leave Chico. I knew at the time it was considered puppy love, but it felt like the real deal. I didn't want to leave my mother, Chico or Morris, but I knew I had to leave that environment. It was for the best, or was it?

CHAPTER 14

THE OTHER SIDE OF ME

I am now 12 years old, almost 13. I have an earring in my nose; I dyed my hair blonde. I'm slim, and oh yeah, I have more than just a nipple now; I have a handful of breasts. I have more street smarts than the average adult. My dad picked me up from my mother's house to go live with him at my Aunt Sue's house. Leaving my mother was a dramatic episode of tears. I performed as if I was going to a funeral.

I arrived at my great Aunt Sue's house with my father. She was my grandmother's sister. My Aunt Sue was beautiful. She had lovely brown skin, thick healthy hair, and big bright brown eyes. She had seven adult children, and four of them were living in the house when I moved in. They were all adults except her daughter Candice who was 16 at the time. Candice was attractive, and she had a son named David. Candice was the only other female in the house besides Aunt Sue. She was not a happy camper, and she disliked everyone. I wondered *why such an attractive girl would be so unattractive on the inside.*

My dad had a room in the attic. He moved out and gave me the room once I moved into the house. He said a girl should always have a room of her own. He announced to the entire house that no one was allowed in my room. Five men were living in the house at the time, including my father. He informed me he was just staying at Aunt Sue's while he saved money, but now that I was there, we would move into our place sooner. In the past, I had been to Aunt Sue's house briefly a few times when I was younger, but I never went past the living room. The house was foreign to me. This was my father's side of the family, and they acted nothing like my mother's side. Soon as I walked into the house, I was ambushed with questions from my Aunt Sue.

"You look just like Desmond. How long will you be here?" Aunt Sue asked.

"Hi, I'm not sure," I gave a phony smirk.

"Oh, I'm asking because Desmond didn't give me any details. He just said his daughter was coming here, and I was shocked," she said. My Aunt Sue immediately asked me a million questions about everything. What happened? How is your mother? Were you enrolled in school?

"Where do you think he got me from? A crack house? Off the street? Oh, I know, maybe I was living in a dumpster?" I sarcastically asked. I wouldn't say I liked her approach, and in my opinion, she was too nosey and judgmental.

"I'm just asking. Just wondering why you had to move with your father suddenly," she said.

"Well, to answer some of your questions, I was enrolled in school. I have an amazing mother. You don't know my story, but I don't want pity or sympathy. For the record, I would much rather be with my mother," I responded in a defensive tone.

"I see you have a smart little mouth on you, oh, and an earring in your nose too?" she stated while looking in my father's direction.

My father frowned his face. He didn't like the earring in my nose, and he thought it was inappropriate for a 12-year-old. I felt my Aunt Sue was asking about the nose ring to be smart. I soon realized my aunt loved to gossip. That's just who she was. Whatever you told her would come back out for sure. Once I realized this, I dealt with her accordingly. We got off on the wrong foot. I was hurt when I first moved in, and I didn't want to be there. As time went on, we eventually created a beautiful relationship.

At first, I would remain silent in the house. I wanted to feel everyone out. I tried to get to know each person's personality. It was hard. These were strangers, and I didn't understand them. I felt so out of place and alone. I gravitated towards baby David; he became my best friend in the house. I was in love with David, and he adored me. My love for David resulted in me trying to reach out to Candice. She rejected me. She called baby David, and I walked him to her room.

"Can he stay with me in the attic sometimes?" I asked.

"You still talking. I don't even like people," she stated. She grabbed David's hand and walked towards her bedroom.

I thought *this is one evil bitch.* She took David and shut her bedroom door. She was too pretty to be acting so mean. Usually, I would try to avoid a negative person, but I wanted to get to know her. I didn't know if it was because she was the only other young girl in the house or because I missed my friends and needed someone to talk to besides myself. One morning I came out of the bathroom as she was walking in. I was looking at the floor without paying attention and bumped into Candice by mistake.

"My bad," I said.

"Oh, you still here?" Candice asked in a sarcastic tone.

"Yup, still here, and I'll still try to talk to you," I said nicely instead of feeling insulted.

"I can see you are going to be an annoying child who doesn't give up," she stated.

"Yup, that's me," I smiled.

This was the day I called a "Candice breakthrough." She wasn't evil, angry, miserable, or a bitch. She was just hurt and had been through some unimaginable things. I sat on her bed, and we opened up to each other about our history of pain. I now understood her hatred towards people. I rubbed all this Sunni love on her and David. She had no choice but to love me. I could now see Candice for the beautiful soul she was, and I completely ignored her sarcastic remarks. I didn't belong in that house, and neither did she. I believe part of being in that house was for me to build a special bond with Candice. I grew to love her and baby David so much.

I missed all my brothers, but I missed Morris the most. Chico was on my mind constantly. He was all I could think about most days. Oh, how I missed my Chico. I worried for my mother; I knew she wasn't doing well without me. I cried a lot. I mean, I really cried. I thought, *why did I leave my mother? I would rather stay in the gutter with her than be without her.* It wasn't personal to my father; I loved him too. I was just attached to my mother as if the umbilical cord was never detached at birth.

My father was sad that I was miserable. He didn't know what to say or how to handle me. The truth is, he didn't know me, and I didn't know him. I missed my mother so much; words couldn't describe the emptiness I felt. I listened to Tupac's song "Dear Mama" every day on repeat. I would start my morning with Tupac blasting on my CD player. I would rap along while finding my clothes to wear for the day, and this was my favorite verse.

"And even though I act crazy
I got to thank the lord that you made me
There are no words that could express how I feel
You never kept a secret, always stayed real
And I appreciate, how you raised me
And all the extra love that you gave me."

My father didn't realize I had grown up. I wasn't that same little baby that stayed at his house all the time when Grandma Pam was alive. I was also a lot more to deal with than the innocent little girl he would randomly get on the weekends. I always loved my father very much, but now I had to get to know him. Understanding him would not be an easy task. He tried to make me comfortable. He bought me a new TV, a cordless phone for the room and new clothes. I thought the phone would be amazing because I could call Chico and Morris. The problem was they would have to actually be home for me to talk to them. Cell phones weren't too popular yet, and most people only had pagers or house phones. I called my mom a lot also, and that became depressing for both of us. We came up with an agreement to only talk once a week so that I could adjust.

I figured it was time I got out of the attic and get to know my family. I probably should have stayed my ass up there. I talked to my Aunt Sue, who happened to love talking. She would tell me everyone's business, even the neighbors. It didn't take long to know everyone's issues. I began to like my aunt. I learned to keep my mouth shut about my business but didn't mind hearing others. I watched the soap opera, "The

Young and the Restless" with Aunt Sue. I learned all the characters and would anxiously wait for the next episode.

My ability to adapt to a new environment is why I always used the motto "I get in where I fit in!" Until now! Oh, there were some issues going on in this house. There was a lot of anger, hate, and hatred toward one another. The secrets slowly came to light. I'll say this, my street issues with my mom were a piece of cake compared to the freaky shit that was going on in this big house. This house was full of pain, animosity, and embarrassing secrets. The grass is not so green on the other side! One day Aunt Sue and I were in the kitchen cutting and eating watermelon.

"Aunt Sue!" yelled an unfamiliar voice.

"I'm in the kitchen," she replied.

The guy walked into the kitchen and hugged me first. It caught me off guard. Watermelon juice was coming down the side of my mouth. "Hi," I said while looking confused.

"Soon as I heard you were here, I came right over. I'm your Uncle Tom, and I was obsessed with you when you were a baby. I carried you everywhere," he said with excitement.

"Oh, I think I remember you a little now. Hi, Uncle Tom," I said. My Uncle Tom was young. He was about 18 years old, caramel complexion, cornrows, and a bright smile.

"I want to talk to you, Niece, when you finish chopping down that watermelon," he said with laughter.

"Okay. Let me take care of this watermelon," I laughed.

I tore that watermelon up. I always loved fruit so much. The only uncle I remembered well was my Uncle Charlie. Uncle Charlie and I were close, and he loved me dearly. By now, his kids had moved to Texas with their mother. I was excited to have another uncle around because uncles were fun. You could love them like a father, but they didn't discipline you like a father. Sounds like a double win to me.

"Uncle Tom, I'm ready," I yelled as I left the kitchen. The words "Uncle Tom" came out of my mouth so naturally. I was just reintroduced to him 15 minutes ago, but I instantly felt like I knew him forever.

"Come out on the front porch," he yelled back.

"You smoke white boys?" I asked. I was enjoying the smell of the weed. I prayed that if I sniffed hard enough, I could catch a contact.

"Girl, what you know about white boys?" he asked.

"I smoke," I admitted. Uncle Tom instantly got quiet. I immediately regret opening up my big mouth and telling him I smoked weed. I looked at him intensely to read his face. I wanted to know if he would tell my father. He then blew out a bunch of smoke and coughed. I laughed.

"Don't be scared. I won't tell on you, Niece," he said. He inhaled another puff of weed.

I took a deep breath and relaxed. "So, are you going to let me hit that white boy or not?" I asked.

"Nope, your father not killing me," he said. He lightly shoved my forehead.

I smiled. I knew I was pushing it, but it had been months since I smoked weed, so it was worth a try. Uncle Tom was the youngest of my grandmother's children, and he seemed to have taken her death the hardest. All my grandmother's kids had a look of sadness in their eyes. After meeting Tom, I realized the sad look I saw in my father's eyes was the same look in all my uncle's and aunts' eyes. It was the look of not having a mother. It was the look of missing something great. The look of loneliness and despair. They all had the same look of no guidance. Uncle Tom and I continued to talk about school, Chico, and the regular catch-up talk. My Uncle Charlie pulled up in his white Cadillac. Aunt Sue had the big family house, so any family member would stop by whenever they wanted.

"Girl, I was looking for you!" Uncle Charlie said. He walked onto the porch with a case of beer.

"For what?" I asked with a smile on my face.

"To give you a big hug," he said as he walked to put his beer down before coming towards me.

I gave my Uncle Charlie a big hug and squeezed him tight. He gave his baby brother Tom a big hug too. Before I knew it, the porch was filled with family. Everyone was smoking weed, laughing, and talking trash. For the first time, I looked around, and I thought, *this is my family, they are a part of me, and I am a part of them.* It felt good, and I finally felt at home. In the back of my mind, I knew I would stay on point. Once I learned the secrets that hid in the walls of this big house, they stayed in my mind. I decided to play along, but I wasn't a fool. I also decided to leave those secrets right in the walls where they resided.

CHAPTER 15

THE TRANSITION

Pops and I had a weird relationship. He loved me more than words could ever express; however, he treated me like I was two years old. I couldn't even walk to the Chinese store at the top of Aunt Sue's block. The way he sheltered me made it hard for me to adjust. I was programmed to have freedom. My mom raised me with morals, and I knew right from wrong. The relationship I had with my mother was built on trust and open communication. It was the complete opposite with my dad because there was no trust or communication. What he said was law, and that was it.

I had a strong enough mind to get out of an unwanted situation. I could've handled situations more effectively than most adults. Unfortunately, my dad didn't know that about me. He didn't know much about me at all. He was worried I would meet a boy that would take me captive as his sex slave and torture me in his dungeon, but I wasn't having sex or even thinking about it. The only boy I thought about was Chico.

My mom's banana and donut demonstration handled that sex thought quite well. I felt like a lion in a cage. My father's strictness made me feel like I was missing something. I wondered *why was he scared for me to walk to the corner alone? What the hell was really going on up there?* I had to get up there to see what could possibly be so dangerous that I couldn't walk to the corner alone. I snuck and walked to the corner, and little behold, there wasn't a damn thing going on.

After a few months, we moved out of Aunt Sue's house. We moved into an apartment in an area called Cedonia. The apartment was nice and designed for privacy. I had a bathroom in my bedroom. My father and his Caucasian girlfriend Jen had their section of the apartment with their bathroom. I had only met my father's new girlfriend, Jen, about three times before we were all living together. Jen was sweet, but she was a little naïve.

Jen had no idea what she was getting herself into with my crazy father and his damaged teenage daughter. She didn't give up on us. I commended her for that because I would've ran for the hills. On top of all that craziness, her family wasn't too thrilled she was dating a black man. None of the obstacles she faced changed her mind about being a part of this new dysfunctional family. She actually married us. I say us because my father and I came as a team. When you marry a man, you marry his kids too. For that, I loved her.

Here's where I got confused. My father had another girlfriend named Mary. My father and I would go to Mary's house throughout the week. For me, it was a break from Aunt Sue's house, and Mary made the best spaghetti with sausages, peppers, parmesan cheese, and buttermilk biscuits.

I asked him about Mary and their relationship, and he claimed to have an open relationship, just friends or some junk that made no sense. Of course, I knew better than to mention one woman to the other. I just wanted to mind my business. Mary got pregnant, and I had the cutest little brother named Mario. I loved that little boy so much. He smelled so new, and I would kiss his little toes. He had red hair like Mary but favored my other siblings and me. Eventually, Mary found out about Jen. I'll just say this; it wasn't pretty!

I still went to school around Aunt Sue's area because she got me enrolled in a good school that was challenging. My father dropped me off every morning. I would catch the public bus to Roland Park Middle School. This was the first school I didn't have to fight. It felt good to be around other kids who just wanted to learn. Most of the kids acted their age.

There were the fake mean girls that all schools had but compared to the rough kids I had encountered; these "mean girls" were clowns to me. I met a set of twins I became close with over the school year. I hung out with them quite often. I don't know why but something always drew me to twins. The school work was challenging at Roland Park, but the atmosphere was easy. I was grateful to have a break from the hood schools. It felt good to just be me without the pressure of watching my back.

I went to Aunt Sue's house every day after school and waited for my dad to pick me up. I would still come over during the summer because my dad and Jen had to work. Uncle Tom was also over there on most days. He asked me to braid his hair. Of course, I did. That became our little thing once he knew I could braid well. My payment would be a puff or two off a joint. It was our little secret. Uncle Tom was a dope rapper, and his skills were sick. He would randomly just spit rhymes. I loved to hear his unique style of rapping. The way he could put words together that made sense was an amazing skill. Off the top of his head, he made up a song called, A

Niece Is a Daughter. I was so hyped about how highly he spoke of me in his music.

He dated a girl named Lizzy, who was different and unique. She was into Tarot card readings and Buddhism. While I braided his hair, we had long talks about whatever was going on with us. He liked Lizzy, but she was much older than him. Aunt Sue was gossiping and in all his business. I knew about Lizzy before he told me from Aunt Sue complaining about her age. Lizzy was friendly, but something was indeed off with her. This time Aunt Sue might have been on to something. I didn't express how I felt to Uncle Tom because he was excited, and I took no pleasure in taking the smile off someone's face. When I finished Uncle Tom's hair, I went into the living room with Aunt Sue.

"Did Tom tell you about his new girlfriend?" Aunt Sue asked.

"Yes," I answered in an annoyed tone. I didn't give her any extra details.

Once she didn't get the details she was looking for; she lost complete interest in that conversation and on to the next talk of the day. She would persistently ask until she got bored. That was her gossip routine. Aunt Sue had no shame in asking whatever she wanted, whenever she wanted, however, she wanted. If she wanted to know something, she asked no matter who was around or who would get offended. Although the gossiping could be annoying, I loved how she stayed true to herself.

Aunt Sue never bit her tongue or took it easy on people to spare their feelings. She did what the hell she wanted to do unapologetically. The funny thing about Aunt Sue was how intelligent she was. She was one of the most brilliant individuals I had ever met. She literally knew every answer on Jeopardy. It was something about being a bold, smart woman that interested me. I stayed away from weak women because they turned me off. I had officially transitioned to the other side.

CHAPTER 16

DON'T TRUST 2 WOMEN IN A WIG

I was watching Jeopardy in Aunt Sue's living room. Before moving in with my father's side of the family, I would never watch Jeopardy. Aunt Sue was molding me into a little old lady. First, it was the "Young and the Restless," then "The Bold and The Beautiful," and then "Jeopardy." Aunt Sue walked into the living room with an excited look on her face.

"Do you want to go to Atlanta with Tam and me this weekend?" Aunt Sue asked.

"This weekend? I doubt my father will let me go."

"Yes, this weekend, we are driving down and leaving at 4:00 in the morning. We would love for you to come," Aunt Sue smiled.

"Can you ask him? I'm sure he won't tell you no," I said as if I came up with a brilliant idea.

"He won't say no. He knows you will be with us," she replied.

Tam was Aunt Sue's oldest daughter. All of Aunt Sue's children had their own looks and did their own thing. I was super excited. I always wanted to visit Atlanta. The only travel experience I had when I was younger was traveling to South Carolina with my grandfather for the summer. When my dad came to pick me up, I was anxious to ask him if I could go to Atlanta. I didn't even bother waiting for Aunt Sue.

"Daddy, can I go to Atlanta with Aunt Sue and Tam?" I eagerly asked

"No!" he immediately responded.

"Why? I will be with Aunt Sue," I pleaded.

"Because I said so!" he said firmly.

"I can't do nothing around here," I said with a high-pitched tone. I pouted and frowned my face. I snatched my book bag from the floor and walked towards the front door.

"Desmond, let her go. We need her to come," Aunt Sue said as she walked into the living room after hearing the commotion.

I didn't understand why she said she needed me to come, but whatever. My father finally agreed. I jumped up and down and I kissed all over his face.

"Thanks, Daddy," I said in a grateful tone.

"Yeah Yeah Yeah," he responded with a smile.

He gave me a couple of hundred dollars, and we rushed home to get some clothes since we were leaving in the middle of the night. When I got home, I rushed and grabbed the worst possible clothes ever. The clothes were tacky, and I didn't understand why I chose them. I guess I figured I would shop when I got there. That night I anxiously laid on Aunt Sue's couch praying we would leave soon because I couldn't get into a deep sleep from excitement. As I lay there half-asleep and half-awake, I felt someone's nasty hand creeping under the covers. The hand was moving slowly and consistently like the itsy-bitsy spider. I took one second to smile at how I was about to fuck this pervert up. I slowly lifted my leg, pulled it back, and kicked with the strongest force a leg could give. The man fell back and held his nose.

"Ouch, got damn it," he lightly screamed.

"Don't fuck with me. I may look like an innocent little girl, but I will kill you without blinking and sleep like a baby," I said while looking him dead in his beady eyes.

"I was just trying to pull the covers over you. You looked cold," he attempted to explain while still holding his nose.

"You heard what I said. Hopefully, we don't have to have this talk again," I said as I pulled the covers back over my body.

Aunt Sue's husband walked away looking slinky and dumb. He was the Devil of this house. These Devils always seem to be somewhere hiding in the shadows waiting to destroy or take some young child's innocence. Sorry Bitch, it won't be me. I lay there for an hour in deep thought. I was insulted that he considered me to be an easy target. He thought I was weak enough to pull that stunt.

I had very little thought about how it made me feel. I dealt with complicated issues by finding a solution right away and then forgetting about it. But was that dealing with it? For me, it was. The energy it took to dwell on any situation is energy lost. I could use that energy to be happy, productive, or have fun. My maturity level as a kid was beyond my years. I didn't think like other children. When put in adult situations, I made adult choices, and I considered the consequences before I reacted.

I didn't mention what happened to anyone because I didn't want the drama or the guilt of sending one of my uncles to jail for taking him out. My father would have killed him without thinking twice. It wasn't worth mentioning because the damage done would outweigh the incident. Plus, he understood the strength of my foot kicking his face, and I'm sure I realized I wouldn't be a good target. He barely had the balls to even look at me again. I felt I handled the situation. Sadly other kids in the family weren't so lucky.

Morning had arrived, it was finally time to get on the road. I was excited and blocked out the creepy hand from the night before. I watched in amazement as we drove from state to state. We stopped in North Carolina and ate at The Cracker Barrel restaurant. We were at the table talking about how the traffic was light because we left so early in the morning. They kept mentioning the name "Sparkle."

"Who is Sparkle?" I finally asked.

"My daughter, your cousin!" Tam exclaimed.

"Oh, I didn't know you had a daughter, Tam. She lives in Georgia?" I asked with a confused look.

"Yes, you'll meet her."

I didn't think too much of this conversation at the time, but I should have. We arrived in Atlanta, Georgia. The atmosphere was beautiful, and the peaches were juicy. The first thing I noticed was the women were shapely. I admired all the thick peach booties walking around. I wasn't a lesbian, but I appreciated a nicely shaped-woman just as much as I enjoyed a well-fit man. The men had gold teeth in their mouths and a colorful style. They looked nothing like the men back home. Everyone seemed to be smiling and happy. The energy in Georgia immediately wore off on me in a good way. We stopped at a store, and everyone was saying, "Hello, hello, hello."

By the time we were done at the store, I was tired of saying hello back to people. Imagine that! You are so accustomed to rude people that you get tired of being friendly. People in Baltimore mostly were angry or just into themselves so much that they didn't take time to greet others. If they said hello to you, they wanted a light for their cigarette, some change, or something selfish. In Baltimore, people walked right past each other without ever opening their mouths to greet one another. Down South was the opposite because they had southern hospitality. I was feeling their vibe. I didn't know how to adapt right away, but I was speaking to everyone by the time we checked into the hotel. Once we got checked in and showered, things got weird. Tam pulled out wigs and sunglasses. She had a short blonde wig, a long black wig, and a red curly wig. She tried them on with different sunglasses.

"Here, Ma, try this one on," Tam told Aunt Sue.

"I'll do the glasses, but I'm not wearing that hideous wig," Aunt Sue responded as she reached for the sunglasses.

"What's up with the wigs?" I asked. They both laughed. I patiently waited for an answer, but instead, they kept talking. I watched Tam try on a long red wig with dark sunglasses.

"That's the one, Tam. That red one looks nice on you," I offered my input.

"Nope, that's too flashy. That one won't work," Aunt Sue interrupted.

"Too flashy?" I asked. I thought, *too flashy? But Tam is flashy! Why would anything be too flashy for Tam? What the hell is going on?*

I was exhausted from the long drive. I tried to convince myself I was full of energy. I slowly felt my eyes drifting. Soon as my eyelids would close, I would pop them back open as if I didn't just doze off. I was too excited to sleep. After a few failed attempts to stay awake, I stopped fighting and went to sleep.

When I woke up, my mouth felt yucky, so I just wanted to brush my teeth. I began looking through my suitcase for my toothbrush when I realized the room was soundless. I figured they fell asleep too. I brushed my teeth and then walked to Aunt Sue's bedroom. She wasn't there. I walked to Tam's area, and she was gone as well. All the wigs were gone, and the rooms were cleaned like they had checked out.

I opened the hotel door and looked up and down the hall as if they would just magically appear. I shut the door and decided not to worry. I went to take a shower. I calmly stood under the hot water and embraced the water hitting my skin. The showerhead was set with force, so the water was coming out with power. I changed the setting and closed my eyes. I talked to God. When the world slowed down and got quiet is when I could hear God the most. I appreciated these moments of silence. Flashes of my life popped into my head, and my mind left the hotel bathroom. I drifted into a world of my past.

The first image was Chico. I pictured his smile and how much I missed him. Then I thought of Morris and our kiss. I smiled at the thought of kissing him. Now I'm back thinking of Chico. I felt sad on the inside, and the water running on my face reminded me of tears. I opened my eyes back to the reality that I was in a shower, in a hotel.

I enjoyed visualizing about my past, so I closed my eyes again. This time, I saw Jazz smiling with her bright, innocent eyes. I instantly started crying, then screaming, then hitting the shower walls. I slid down to the shower floor and cried while the water hit my naked body. I let out all the pain I held in, then I talked to myself and yelled out loud, *GET YOUR ASS UP. YOU ARE STRONGER THAN THIS. THE PITY PARTY IS OVER!*

I slowly stood up and took the soap, and rubbed it in the washcloth. I slowly washed my arm while silently sobbing. I thought *girl get yourself together. You are in the ATL to have fun.* That fast, my mind switched back to reality. I was ready to have some fun. These awkward moments in the shower were my therapy. I never received professional help, so I coped the best way I knew how. Screaming and crying seem to work. I continued to wash up, and I started singing "Can We Talk?" by Tevin Campbell.

> *"Last night I... I saw you standing*
> *And I started... started pretending*
> *I knew you, and you knew me too*
> *And just like a roni...you were too shy*
> *But you weren't the only cause, so was I*
> *And I've dreamed of you ever since*
> *Now I've built up my confidence*
> *Girl next...next time you come my way*
> *I'll know just what to say*
> *Can we talk for a minute...girl*
> *I want to know your name."*

My singing was interrupted when I heard screaming. "Girl, you singing, aren't you?" Tam yelled.

"You know I got the voice," I laughed, but I instantly felt relieved they were back.

"Hurry up Sunni before the water gets cold," Aunt Sue demanded.

I snickered to myself because the water was already getting cold. I was in the shower for at least 45 minutes. We got dressed for dinner. I made the horrible mistake of ordering a crab cake. I knew better. Maryland is known for our crabs, so why would I expect a decent crab cake from down South? I complained, but I ate it. We got back to the hotel. Tam and Aunt Sue shut their bedroom door and were whispering. I thought again, *what is up with them?* The next morning, I woke up eager to start our day in the "A." When I came to the living room area, Tam was already up looking in the yellow pages. I thought maybe she was trying to find us something to do for the day, so I didn't overthink it.

We went to breakfast and got a nice southern meal. It was so much food—biscuits with gravy, waffles, grits, eggs, home fries, bacon, ham, and sausage. I thought, *no wonder all these chicks have big butts; they are eating well down here!* Back home, all I would've got for the same price was a bacon, egg, and cheese on toast. We then did a little shopping at The Underground. The Underground is a mall under the ground. I bought a nice new outfit that my dad would disapprove of for sure. I planned on wearing it later that night so he would never have the chance to see it. According to our travel plans, we had one more day in Atlanta, and then we would leave in the morning. Later, around 1:00 p.m., we drove around a residential area. We kept riding around in circles.

"Why are we here?" I asked.

"Tam thinking about moving down here, we are just looking," Aunt Sue replied.

"You love to move around, Tam. I don't blame you," I replied. Tam was the type to live her life to the fullest. She would pick up and move to another state without a second thought. We went back to the hotel, and Tam put on the wig and sunglasses she had earlier. Aunt Sue only put on a pair of sunglasses.

"Okay, Bonnie and Clyde. You two are up to something, but I'm tired of guessing, so I'm going to take a nap," I proceeded to walk to my room.

"No, girl, you are coming with us! Make sure you pack all your stuff too, in case we want to check out early," Tam yelled.

I was so confused, but I did as she said. I thought of calling my father to tell him they were acting weird, but I didn't. I questioned for a split second, *are they going to sell me for sex trade?* The moment the thought crossed my mind, I laughed because that was silly. No way they would do something crazy like that. We got in the car and drove 20 minutes back to a residential neighborhood. By now, I knew to keep quiet and stop asking questions. We drove around the same area maybe three or four times and finally I saw a school. Tam parked the car on the side street of the school.

"Why are we at this school?" I asked. The curiosity was killing me.

"We need you to ask Sparkle to come with you to the car," Aunt Sue said.

"What! She doesn't know me. Why would she come to the car with me? Tam, why can't you go get her?" I exclaimed.

"Her father is stupid and told her some junk, but she loves her grandmother, and she will come to the car if you tell her that her grandmother is in the car," Tam explained calmly.

"I'll stand outside of the car if she doesn't come, and then she will see me," Aunt Sue said in a convincing tone.

"Alright, I'll get her, but I don't understand why you or Aunt Sue can't get her," I boldly stated to Tam as I opened the car door. My common sense told me something about this didn't sound right. When the school bell rang, kids were running everywhere. It was the last day of school in Georgia. Tam searched and searched.

"Sunni, there she goes, pink shirt!" Tam yelled in an anxious voice.

"With the blue bookbag?" I asked. Tam nodded her head yes. I nervously walked towards Sparkle. She looked about my age. She was light with brown hair, almost red hair, and a charming face. I walked up to Sparkle and stopped right in front of her.

"Hi, are you Sparkle?" I nervously asked.

"Yeah, I'm her. Who are you?" she asked in a country accent. She looked me up and down. She knew from the moment she heard me talk I wasn't from the South.

"I'm your cousin, your grandmother Sue wants to see you," I said.

"Where is she?" she asked. Her eyes were bright with excitement, but I could tell she didn't trust me.

"She's over there," I pointed to the car, and Aunt Sue stepped out and waved her hand. Sparkle waved back with a big smile on her face.

"Wait, I have to get my little sister first. We always walk home together," she demanded.

I didn't know what to say. I froze and looked at Aunt Sue for help. I didn't even know why I was asking her to the car in the first place. The entire situation made me uncomfortable. Luckily Aunt Sue caught my reaction when Sparkle was about to walk away. Aunt sue happily waved her hands to motion Sparkle to come over to her. Sparkle looked suspicious but walked towards the car. Soon as Sparkle got close enough to the car, Aunt Sue hugged her tight.

"Your dad already picked up your sister. He knows I'm coming to take you home so we could talk while I'm in town," Aunt Sue lied.

"You sure?" Sparkle asked.

"Yes, don't worry. You are so big and pretty now. Are you hungry?" Aunt Sue asked to put Sparkle's mind at ease.

"Yes, I'm starving," Sparkle said as she rubbed her stomach. We all got in the car.

"I'm hungry too," I added.

"I didn't know my mother was with you," Sparkle said in an intense voice. Her face looked worried.

"Hi Sparkle, I missed you," Tam said with a bit of sarcasm.

"Hi Ma," she nonchalantly responded.

"Where are we eating?" I asked. No one responded.

"You sure my father picked up my little sister? I always walk her home," Sparkle asked her grandmother Sue.

"Yes, she is safe," Tam quickly answered.

"No one asked you," Sparkle mumbled under her breath. She looked in my direction for clarity. I remained quiet and wondered, *where was her little sister?*

"And what's your name again?" Sparkle asked me in a suspicious tone.

"I'm Sunni, Desmond's daughter," I replied nicely. We drove for about twenty minutes, and before long, we were on the highway.

"We could have gotten food close to my house. This is in the opposite direction," Sparkle yelled.

No one answered. Sparkle and I kept talking in the back of the car. She told me she was 11 years old, and she loved living in Georgia and how fun it was. She said she had a sexy boyfriend that she had been dating since the 5th grade. She told me her little sister was her best friend and how much southern fun they had. I told her I recently moved with my dad and was getting to know this side of the family. She rolled her eyes a little at her mother.

"Fathers are fun, and they spoil you," Sparkle said loud enough for her mother to hear her.

"I don't know because I'm a momma's girl, and I'm just getting the hang of this daddy thing," I responded. Another twenty minutes passed, and Sparkle looked at her mother.

"You are not taking me back home, are you?" she bluntly asked her mother. By this time, I too had realized we kidnapped Sparkle.

"Nope, you are coming back to Baltimore with me," Tam replied with no emotion.

"I don't want to go with you! My father will be so worried. They will think I went missing," she screamed. She cried hysterically. I tried to console her.

"Don't touch me. I wish I never trusted you. You are evil just like them," she screamed at me.

"Sorry, I didn't know. I didn't realize we would even see you until today," I explained.

"Don't talk to me. I hate them, and I hate you too," Sparkle said as she wept.

I left her alone. Every hour or so, she would try to open the door while the car was moving, but the child lock was on. She would randomly scream, "Let me out of this car!" It was a long 10-hour trip home full of drama. Weirdly enough being in a car for so many hours, you forgive quickly. Sparkle talked to me after about 4 hours. I told her again I didn't know about the setup. Once we got close to Baltimore, Tam let Sparkle call her father, and Sparkle was so relieved. In the end, she believed me, but we both learned not to trust two women in wigs and sunglasses.

CHAPTER 17

ONE MUST FIX THEIR MISTAKES

Sparkle and I hung out every weekend and became close. Sparkle constantly talked about Georgia and how she missed her family and friends. I had a lot of guilt I couldn't let go. Although I didn't know the intentions of the trip to Georgia, it didn't stop me from feeling guilty. Not only did we kidnap the poor girl, but we also dragged her back to Baltimore, where she constantly got into fights. She was sweet and southern, and Baltimore was cold and harsh. It wasn't a good fit for her.

Tam was popular in the party scene, so I went to their house every other weekend to stay with Sparkle while Tam sold clothes to the strippers in DC. We had a ball. Tam was a free spirit, and I admired her ability to live freely. She moved wherever she wanted to move and did whatever she wanted to do. She spontaneously lived her life. In my mind, I would grow up to be the kind of woman who lived her life and did not do what society says she must do. Although I admired Tam's "Don't Give A Fuck Lifestyle," it was inappropriate for Sparkle.

She was used to stability, and Tam was not a 9-5, cook dinner every night type of chick. Tam was a clubber. On the weekends that I didn't go to Tam's house; Sparkle came to my house. Our parents agreed to rotate.

Sparkle eventually adjusted to Maryland, but she was sad. We talked intimately about how we missed our other parents. I missed my Queen, and she missed her father. We would be in my room listening to "Bone Thugs and Harmony." She had never heard this kind of music down South. I loved Bone. I also had an old heart. That's what Granddaddy would tell me when I would sing along to all his oldie but goodie songs. The first time I played the Temptations song "Ain't Too Proud to Beg," Sparkle almost fainted.

"You are so old! Why are you listening to these old people's songs?" Sparkle asked.

"Girl, you don't know about good music!" I responded.

"It's good Sunni if you are over fifty!" she said with laughter and annoyance in her voice.

"I know you want to leave me, But I refuse to let you go, If I have to beg, plead for your sympathy, I don't mind 'cause you mean that much to me. Ain't too proud to beg, and you know it, please don't leave me, girl,"

I sang and grabbed her arm as if she was my woman and I was David Ruffin. We both laughed. The following weekend Sparkle came over, guess what she wanted to hear? "The Temptations!" Her favorite song was "My Girl." I smiled at the influence I had on her. She was like my little sister. I showed her how to braid, and it amazed her when she successfully did her first cornrow. Unfortunately, no matter how connected we were, Sparkle still had a sadness to her. She was still incomplete and missed her family. I understood because I missed my old life too.

Uncle Tom and his band came over to our house to record a song. Uncle Charlie came over too with a case of beer. Sparkle and I were excited to have entertainment in the home. My dad was becoming very involved in their music. He believed in Uncle Tom and his skills. My father made our apartment into a music studio on the weekend. He would help with the equipment or whatever he could do. We all believed in their dream to make it.

The group was different, and their style of rap was unique. Uncle Tom and his rap group didn't rap about money, hoes, and bitches. They rapped about real-life relatable situations, and their chemistry as a group was spot on. The rhythm of their flow was very cohesive. All they needed was a big break.

"Niece, you trying to write a verse and hop on this beat?" Uncle Tom asked me.

"Nah, Unc, I don't have no skills, but Sparkle has a little something going on," I said.

"I'm shy. We will just listen," Sparkle responded. She had a pleasant voice, and she could rap.

I watched my uncle in admiration as he flowed the words out of his mouth so naturally. He would look up at me and smile. When no one was looking, I gave him the signal to sneak me a puff or two of some weed. He shook his head no. I thought, *dag he not even going to try to sneak me some.* Later I found a half of joint wrapped up in my private bathroom. I smiled from ear to ear with anticipation of lighting up. I thought to myself, *I have the coolest uncle ever.*

Uncle Charlie was my favorite, but Uncle Tom was young and more relatable. Uncle Charlie always treated me like his own daughter. I mean, you could see the love in his eyes for me. Our bond was crazy strong. I loved him almost as much as I loved my father. The only reason I loved my father a little more is because I came out of his balls; otherwise, their love would be equal. Uncle Tom was coming for Uncle Charlie's spot, and he was coming strong. It's nothing like uncles. It's like you have multiple fathers to spoil you. As the night calmed down, everyone went home. Sparkle and I took showers for bed. We lay there side by side in my queen-sized bed.

"I have to tell you something. I don't know how you will feel about it," Sparkle said.

"Just tell me, whatever it is, we can work it out," I replied.

"I'm scared to tell you. You will be mad," Sparkle said fearfully.

"Why would I be mad? Just say it Spark!" I responded. I was getting annoyed. I just wanted her to spit it out already.

"My grandmother on my father's side purchased me a plane ticket to go back to Georgia tomorrow," she said in a low tone.

"What? Tomorrow?" I questioned.

"I wasn't going to tell you, I would've just been gone tomorrow, but I couldn't do that to you," she said with sympathy.

"Although I will miss you, I know you are depressed here. So, since I helped kidnap you, I will help you escape," I whispered.

I instantly felt sad. Spark was my baby, and she made my days much brighter. I became really attached to her. She was the only girl in the family in my age range that I had built a close relationship with. She also gave me something to look forward to every weekend. When she left, I knew my life would go back to the long, dull days with no one to talk to or nothing to do. My father was strict, and he never wanted me out of his eyesight unless I was with Sparkle. My freedom would leave with Sparkle, and I dreaded it. Spark and I came up with a plan. When my father left for work, we would call her a cab to go to her grandmother's, who would then take her to the airport. Her flight left early in the day.

"I don't want to leave it all on you. Everyone will be so mad at you," Spark said with her head hung low.

"I know they'll be mad, and I'm sure I'll get in trouble, but I'll take the fall for you. I love you, and you will always be my little baby," I assured her.

"I'll write a note addressed to you saying I ran away, don't look for me, and I love you," Sparkle suggested.

"Okay, the note will do," I softly cried. I couldn't hold back my tears any longer. Sparkle cried too. We decided I would act like I was asleep, and when I woke up, she was gone. That's exactly what we did. Just as fast as Sparkle came in, my life is just as fast as she left. Once I knew Sparkle was on her way to the airport, I called Aunt Sue.

"Hello," she answered.

"Sparkle is gone! She left me a note. I was asleep, and when I woke up, she was gone!" I yelled in a panicked voice.

"What? Wait, let me click over and call her mother!" she said. Aunt Sue clicked over and called Tam. My heart was racing as Tam's phone rang. I prayed she didn't answer, but she did. I told her the same story.

"THAT'S BULLSHIT. YOU ARE FUCKING LYING!" Tam yelled.

I held the phone while she cursed me out. Then my father punished me. I had to repeat the story like ten times for every family member who called, asking, "What happened again?" I never changed the story. It didn't matter. I still got in trouble and decided I had to take one for the team. I learned in life; one must fix their mistakes, especially if the mistake caused someone to be unhappy.

CHAPTER 18

THINGS WILL NEVER BE THE SAME

Uncle Tom was going through some relationship issues with his girlfriend, Lizzy. Their relationship was on and off, and it started affecting him. He stayed at Aunt Sue's house more and more. Uncle Tom had a natural sense of calmness and sadness about him. On this day my family went to the beach, it was about 30 of us. I saw Uncle Tom acting distant and kind of staying to himself. He sat in a chair alone and far away from everyone else. I left the crowd and walked over to him.

"Who's my favorite uncle?" I asked in a peppy voice.

Charlie is. Then me," Uncle Tom responded

"I love y'all equally," I laughed. Everyone knew Uncle Charlie was my favorite.

"Yeah, yeah, niece," he gave me a half-smile.

"You seem down. Do you want to take a walk? They have a trail area over there," I suggested.

"I would love that. We can just get away from everyone for a minute," Uncle Tom agreed.

"Daddy, me and Uncle Tom will be back!" I yelled to my father. I put my beach bag down on a chair.

"Where y'all going?" my father asked.

"For a quick walk," I answered.

"Okay, come back before the food gets off the grill," he yelled. I nodded my head, and we walked away towards the trail.

"What's bothering you Uncle," I asked.

"Just life, Niece. I'm lonely too."

"If things are not working out with you and Lizzy, it's okay. You know someone will come along and love you the way you deserve to be loved," I said with encouragement.

"It's not just her. It's life, and no one can ever give me the love I need. I need my mother's love."

"I miss my mother's love too," I said, although it was no comparison because my mother was still alive.

"Do you ever wonder why are we even here? Everything is so hard, and for what?" he asked.

"Yes, I have wondered that. I also wondered why God let certain things happen. But I also know we are here for special moments just like the one me and you are sharing right now."

"You are smarter than most adults, and I love you, Sunni, always know that!"

"I love you too, Uncle Tom, always know that! Now pass that joint and let me sneak a puff," I laughed.

"One puff only!" he said as he handed me the joint.

"Okay, one puff," I sucked in the deepest inhale my lungs could handle. Then I took an extra puff and took off running with his joint. He chased me, and I was running and puffing. We laughed so hard.

"You run like a turtle," I yelled.

"You better act normal when we get back, or your father will kill me!" he fussed.

We walked back to the beach, laughing and talking. Uncle Tom's sadness had left, and that made me feel good. We had so much fun, we ate, dunked each other under the water, and chilled in the sun. It was a good family day. Some time went by, and my father and I were on our way to the market.

"Let's stop by Aunt Sue's house first," he stated.

"Why? I thought we were going straight home," I responded in an annoyed voice. I didn't feel like stopping at Aunt Sue's. It was a weekday, and I was on my menstrual cycle.

When we got there, Uncle Tom was on the porch, and he looked upset. He had broken up with his girlfriend again. I walked up to him and gave him a tight hug. He hugged me back and said, "Hey, Niece." There was also some other tension going on, but I didn't stay on the porch to listen. I went straight into Aunt Sue's house to ask her what was going on with the soap operas. Since I was in school during the daytime, Aunt Sue had to fill me in on all the soap opera dramas. After about thirty minutes, I heard my father calling me.

"Sunni, come on!" he yelled so I could hear him from the front porch.

"I'm coming," I yelled back. I gave Aunt Sue a hug and a kiss on the cheek. I walked onto the front porch.

"Tom is coming to our house tonight," he informed me.

I got excited. We drove home, and I heard them talking about his girlfriend and other issues he was having at Aunt Sue's house. I blocked out their conversation. I didn't pay them any mind. I was daydreaming. Being my mother's only child often left me using my imagination. I loved talking to myself and living in a fantasy world. I could block out a room full of people and take myself far away from reality into a dream world. That's where I was in the back seat of my father's car; I was in my own little dream world.

We got to the house, and Jen my father's wife was away working for the week. She worked out of town with disabled kids. She only returned home on the weekends. My dad cut the music up super loud, and he and Uncle Tom drank beer and talked trash. I went straight to my room for a nice hot bath. When I finished, I came into the living room to talk for a while.

Uncle Tom was rapping, and we were all laughing and having a good time. It was getting late, and my eyes were heavy. I looked at Uncle Tom, and he appeared to be getting better. He didn't look so down anymore. He was smiling and talking to my father. For some reason, I captured his smile in my mind. I kissed my Uncle Tom on the cheek and walked over to my dad to kiss him too. I told them both I loved them, and I went to bed. The next morning my dad and I got dressed for work and school. My dad woke Uncle Tom up.

"Do you want to stay here for the day or go back to the city because we'll be out all day?" My father asked Uncle Tom.

"I'll stay here and work on some music if that's cool?" he replied.

"Of course. You can lie on my bed if you want," my father suggested.

"Nah, I'm good, you know me," Uncle Tom replied.

"You love laying on the floor, don't you?" I asked Uncle Tom.

"Yup, you know it, Niece. Bro, I'll actually stay here for a couple of days, if you don't mind?" Uncle Tom asked.

"Hell no, I don't mind. You know my home is your home. See you later," my father said.

"Love you, Uncle," I said to Uncle Tom, and we left. That evening when we got home, my father went to the apartment first while I grabbed some bags out of the car. I heard him yelling when I entered the apartment.

"Tom!" my father screamed. Uncle Tom didn't answer. I went to the kitchen to put the bags on the counter.

"Boy, get up. You didn't hear me calling you?" my father asked.

"Daddy! Are there any more bags?" I asked. I went towards my father's room to jump on Uncle Tom, but I heard my father scream before I got there.

"NO NO NO! FUCK!" he yelled.

"Daddy!" I screamed. My heart immediately dropped. I looked in my dad's room and saw Uncle Tom's foot as if he was lying on the floor asleep as always. Before I could walk closer, my father stopped me.

"Don't come in here!" he said in a weak but aggressive tone. My father's tone made me panic.

"Daddy, what's wrong? Please say something," I asked. My father didn't respond. Instead, he hit the wall multiple times. I got a little closer and saw Uncle Tom lying on the floor, but my father pushed me back before I could get closer.

"TOM, GET UP! GET UP! GET UP! PLEASEEEEE, PLEASEEEEE GET UP, UNCLE TOM PLEASE! UNCLE TOM, PLEASE! PLEASE GET UP! WHY IS HE NOT MOVING? TOM PLEASE GET UP! PLEASEEEEE!" I screamed and yelled as tears and drool filled my face.

Uncle Tom did not move. Uncle Tom did not get up. I immediately thought back to earlier that day and the night before. I remembered his smile that I captured in my mind. My father's touch snapped me out of my thoughts. He was now hugging me and crying too. We went into the apartment hallway; our neighbors came out. My father asked them a series of questions, *did they hear anything? What happened to my fucking brother? That's my baby brother in there! What the fuck happened?* No one responded. He cried and punched another wall. I became quiet. I needed a minute to stop all my thoughts. I became numb. So numb. I lost all feeling. I cried quietly, and I stay paralyzed. A neighbor called the police. Another neighbor walked over to me.

"Sweetheart, get up," the woman said.

I ignored her. I ignored them all. I wanted my Uncle Tom to get off that fucking floor and give me a hug. I wanted to wake up from this nightmare. I needed one more kiss, one more hug, one more walk, one more talk but more than anything. I needed him to get up off that fucking floor! But he wouldn't. He would never be here again.

I lost my uncle to depression. My uncle made a choice to commit suicide and leave us all behind to deal with the pain and grief of never seeing his precious face again. I begged the funeral home to let me braid his hair because he wouldn't want them to braid it. They agreed at first but later changed their mind because of the gunshot wound.

Uncle Tom didn't leave a traditional suicide letter. Instead, he wrote a suicide rap song where he explained his reasoning. I wasn't allowed to read the lyrics. I have now lost my last piece of innocence on this day. Death has shown up again, but this time with a vengeance. I was forever changed. I would never be the girl I was before that day. My father would never be the man he was either. The look on his face is a look I never witnessed. That day is the day I officially became a DAMAGED Little Girl!

CHAPTER 19

FUCK BEING GOOD

Time will heal, so they say. My family needs time to hurry the fuck up and heal us. My father was in a bad place mentally, and he wasn't doing well with the grieving process. Living in that apartment after Uncle Tom's death was hell. It was cold all the time, with a permanent chill in the air. I would cut the kitchen light off, and by the time I got in my room, the light would be back on. Our front door was wide open almost every night. People would walk right into our apartment and yell, "Your door is open again." The gloomy presence over the apartment became unbearable.

This was a different type of death. This was a chosen death, and grieving works differently when a person decides to leave his loved ones behind. It left us to think about what could've been done differently. *Why didn't we help him more? Were there signs we ignored? Was he crying out for help?* So much left for the wandering mind to think of. Our apartment became overwhelming, so after a few months, we moved out. We couldn't take the vibes anymore. That experience made me believe in spirits and the afterlife. The weird things that occurred at the apartment made the grieving process worse.

We moved into a house close to Garrison Blvd that my dad and Jen bought. We got an American bulldog; my father named him Tom. He was a wild dog, and he loved me a lot, maybe too much. The dog annoyed me with his unruly behavior. The last thing I wanted most nights was an overly excited dog jumping and licking all over me, knocking me down. He was strong and aggressive.

I pretended to be happy about getting a dog since my father thought it would help us feel better. Jen became pregnant with my little brother. We all tried to be joyful, but we had unresolved issues. We needed therapy. Nothing was the same after Tom's death. One cold night we all sat around the house bored and quiet. My father tried to break the ice, so he turned on some music.

"Come on, baby girl, come dance with your pops," he said as he reached his arm out for me.

"No, Daddy!" I smiled.

He grabbed my arms and swung me around. I laughed, and we slowly danced to Luther Vandross's song "Here and Now." It was a beautiful moment during a dark time. It was moments like these that we lived for. I loved my father, and at that moment, I realized how much he loved me. We just didn't know how to communicate as father and daughter. I started to understand that death hurts but not living hurts more. So that day, while dancing with my handsome father, I decided to stop being sad about Uncle Tom and start living.

Who did I think I was? Oh, I thought I would be able to just live like a typical teenager? I thought I could escape grief? Maybe, I thought I could have normal teenage problems like my acrylic nail chipping or maybe some stupid boy who wouldn't like me at school. NOPE, not me! I'm not that lucky because "Life's a BITCH, and then you DIE." Two weeks after moving into the new house, I got a phone call, and my dad handed me the phone with a sad look on his face. I took the phone with hesitation.

"Hello. Ma, calm down. I can't understand you. What's wrong?" I asked. All I heard on the other end of the phone was sobbing.

"Sunni, Morris passed away. I'm so sorry. I know how much you loved him," she stuttered.

I dropped the phone and just screamed. There I lay on the floor in a puddle of tears. This puddle just keeps growing. I had flashbacks of Morris's face. I thought of him sleeping in my bed because he was too drunk to make it home; I reminisced on all the fun times, mainly when Honey and Morris were joking with each other; I thought of the times we wrested and had paintball fights; I thought of the late-night talks when everyone was asleep; I thought of the day the police beat him up and how bad I wanted to help him. But lastly, I thought of the kiss we swore to never talk about again.

Yup, I had lost my friend. Morris was now deceased. He was now another dead face on a t-shirt. He's another face on an obituary that will hang up on my mirror. Now I'm pissed with God. *What did I ever do to deserve all this death? Why even let me love people if they will just be snatched away?* My mom told me Morris had gotten into a fight, and he won. Unfortunately, the guy didn't take the ass-whooping lightly, so he got off the ground and shot him.

Now I was at the lowest possible place to be. I had to go to yet another funeral and say goodbye to yet another person I loved. God owes me an explanation. Yes, everyone must die, but why must I lose everyone. I was mad at God, and our relationship was getting weak. I lost faith in the process. I started to hate life because the moment I started living, the shadow of death came right back for me. I went to Morris' funeral and saw all the guys, and we all cried together at his casket. None of them had too much pride about being a man crying in public. They loved Morris, and we needed to cry, so we did. We went to the gravesite, and as all the cars started to leave, someone played the song "Crossroads" by Bone Thugs-N-Harmony. I remember thinking, *FUCK! Morris is gone!*

I was tired of being a good girl. What was being good getting me? My dad didn't trust me. God kept snatching people away! I didn't have my Queen. Frankly, I was tired of trying to figure out this shitty place called life. After Morris's funeral, my relationship with my father got worse. I was so angry. I barely had time to deal with Uncle Tom's death, and that double blow of death took me over the edge.

Honestly, my dad was angry too, and losing his little brother caused him a lot of guilt and pain. I think he felt we shouldn't have left Tom in the house that day. Or maybe we shouldn't have picked him up in the first place. Who knows what could have gone differently if we made a different choice. Either way, at this point, we were not getting along. I was ready to break free of the cage he had me in like a lost lion. A lion rules his jungle, and I was ready to rule mines.

I got back in touch with Honey after Morris's death. I somehow convinced my dad to let me go to her house every other weekend. Honey lived in O'Donnell Heights projects. The atmosphere was totally different from Perkins Projects. It was more country and quieter. I was so happy to be with Honey. When I walked into her house, I immediately picked up my niece Hazel; she had beautiful hazel eyes with long eyelashes and the cutest face. She was the perfect mixture of

Rell and Honey. My two nephews also jumped on me for some love. I kissed all over them. This was my first-time meeting Hazel, so I gave her a little extra love. The last time I saw Honey, she was pregnant with Hazel.

Let the party begin! It was time to smoke weed and feel good. It was time to forget about all that death and start living, right? I was tired of crying! I deserved to live a little. Although Honey loved me and was older, she didn't know how to be a good role model. Honey just wanted me to have fun with her because she looked at me like her best friend instead of a little sister.

So much fun we had. I went to Honey's every chance I got; it was like I got a piece of my old self back. My hood self. The hood was exciting. It was always something going on, or someone's house to have fun in, some weed to smoke, or some music to dance to. I was having fun and doing everything except having sex. I was still a virgin, but not for long.

I became interested in boys. I had gotten this tingly fire inside my girl. I called my vagina "My Girl." She was mine, and I loved her. I started talking to a guy named Moo, he was 16 years old, and I was 14. Moo liked me and was stuck under me like glue. When I moved, he moved as if he was my clone. Chico was the last boy I was hugged up with and the only boy I had a genuine connection with.

Unfortunately, Chico's number was disconnected, and we lost contact around the time my uncle died. Moo was no Chico. I knew no one would be my Chico, so I didn't expect that kind of love. I also knew Chico, and I couldn't be together because we lived so far apart. We were young and not mature enough to wait for each other. That would be unrealistic, but our love never died.

There were no stores in O'Donnell Heights, so we had to walk through the entire project to get to a gas station or wait for the truck. The truck sold everything like a store, bread, eggs, chips, soda, bacon, etc. When the truck came, I asked Moo for $2 for a soda and some chips. I always had my own money. My father always made sure I didn't have to ask anyone for anything. I didn't consider $2 to be money that was more like loose change you find in a car.

"I'll get it for you, babe," Moo said as he walked outside to the truck.

"Funyuns, not Doritos," I yelled across the street as I stood in Honey's doorway. I went back into the house and grabbed the remote, and plopped down on the sofa.

"Get a cup out of the kitchen Boo," Moo said. He came back with one soda and one bag of Funyuns. I thought nothing of it because that's what I asked for.

"A cup for what?" I asked.

"So we can share this soda," Moo stated as if I asked a dumb question.

"You are joking, right?" I laughed.

"No, Boo. What you too good to share a soda and some chips with your man?" he seriously asked.

"Clearly, you don't know me, Moo. #1 you are not my man, #2 I don't share spitty sodas, #3 you are cheap because you have a pocket full of drug money and didn't buy yourself a soda for your dry ass throat. I don't deal with cheap dudes. You can leave."

"What? You are an ungrateful ass Bitch," he cursed and yelled.

"Get the fuck out and take your soda and chips with you. Cheap Bitch!" I barked back.

I so badly wanted to knock him upside the head with the remote that was still in my hand. The thought crossed my mind quite a few times to just hit him. I learned what kind of provider I needed from my parents. My mother never had a man around her who didn't provide. My father was a provider and a protector as well. I didn't deal with lames. I definitely wasn't about to be hugged up with someone who can't feed me or quench my thirst. Nope, not me. When a girl has a father, her expectations are higher! She expects more, she wants more, and she feels she deserves more. Bye Moo! A few weeks went by, and I met this guy named Enrique through Honey.

"Girl, you should talk to Enrique. He is so cute," Honey said with excitement.

"His name is Enrique? What is he mixed or something?" I asked.

"Spanish and Black. Girl, he is hot," she exclaimed.

When I first saw him, I was surprised at how attractive he was. Honey introduced us, and although he was handsome, he didn't have much personality. He was actually quite rude. I didn't care for his disrespectful attitude, handsome or not. The second time I met him, he was drunk and very flirtatious. To be honest, it flattered me. He was easy on the eyes, so that wasn't the issue. The issue was his attitude.

We all hung out that night talking trash and smoking weed. I didn't like to drink. I wasn't a fan of the taste of alcohol, but Honey always pushed it on me for some reason. Out of the blue, I felt sick and wheezy. I left Honey and went back to her house. I took a shower and lay in the bed. I was super high, and the weed made me dizzy, or maybe it was that shot of awful alcohol I barely got down. I dozed off and woke up to someone kissing my neck.

"What the fuck!" I yelled as I pushed the hot lips off my neck. I opened my eyes, and I realized it was Enrique.

"Damn girl, calm down," he said as he tried to continue to kiss my neck.

"What are you doing in here?" I asked with an attitude.

"I'm spending the night with you, Boo," he whispered.

"Get out! I'm sleepy," I demanded.

"Chill, I'm not going to bite you," he said calmly.

"You are not getting none of my girl, so don't touch me. You can just lay there," I demanded. I was irritated and just wanted to go back to sleep, nor did I feel like arguing with his rude ass.

"I'm just sleepy too. I won't bother you," Enrique quickly lied.

I wondered, *how the fuck did he get in here anyway?* I went back to sleep with his arms around me. I woke up to kisses on my neck again. This time I was more aware. The kisses kind of tickled, so I lightly laughed. It felt weird. I told him to stop a few times but not forcefully. I tried to fight what I knew was about to happen. I kind of didn't want him to stop. He began to undress me, and I lay there, letting him take control.

"I'm a virgin," I whispered.

"Me too!" he paused.

"No, I'm serious," I said. I didn't know if he was being sarcastic or if he was really a virgin too.

"Me too, Sunni. I'm serious too!" he proclaimed.

He then took off his shirt. His dark mixed skin was beautiful, and his abs were perfectly formed. He smelled like cologne and Hennessy. He pulled out a condom. When I saw the condom wrapper, I got scared. My heart was thumping, and my girl was thumping too. I thought, *what is this feeling? Why is my adrenaline out of control right now?* I was too scared to look at his penis, so when he put the condom on, I turned my head. My legs trembled as he slowly dragged his body in between my legs. We were face to face, and his body was on top of mine. His body was hot like a fever, and my mind was racing with fear. He rubbed his penis around my girl. I jumped back.

"It's okay, I'll go slow," he whispered.

"Please," I pleaded.

I felt an immediate sense of relief knowing that he would go slow. Enrique moved his penis around my girl again and breathed slowly and heavily on my neck. His slow breathing allowed me to relax. He lightly kissed my neck and entered my kingdom of juices slowly but with force. It felt like my girl was ripping. It was so painful for the first few strokes, and then it calmed down. It was the worst sex of my life! He came after the 10th stroke, and BOOM, it was over! (yes, I counted the strokes, what else is there to do while I lay there in painful boredom?) He pulled his limp dick out of me.

"Damn, that was good," he said. Then he immediately fell over and started snoring. He didn't even bother to remove the condom. I wanted to put his ass out, but I was confused. I thought, *what the fuck was that? Was that sex? Maybe I just lacked experience. Maybe that's how it should've felt. Maybe everyone hyped this sex shit up, and it's all bullshit.* He snored loudly like a drunk man. I moved his heavy arm from around me, rolled my eyes, and left him there asleep.

I went into the bathroom to wash up. There was liquid running down my legs, and I panicked, thinking maybe the condom burst. I smelled the liquid and realized it was my juices, and I calmed down. I looked all inside my girl, and she was red, swollen, and a little sore. I was so fucking mad at myself. I lost my virginity to a ten-pump, Hennessy-smelling, limp dick ass, sexy Black- A- Rican. I didn't understand why Honey let him in, and she knew I was asleep. I was more upset with myself for being weak. I went downstairs to find Honey. It was like 4 in the morning, and she was up talking to one of her homeboys.

"Honey, I need to talk to you," I demanded. I told her what happened and how I didn't like sex. I honestly wanted her to discipline me and tell me never to do it again. Instead, she started asking questions.

"Did you use a condom? How big was it?" she asked

"Yes, we used a condom. It looked little when it came out, but it was kind of soft."

"Did you switch positions? Did he do it slowly or fast? Did he do any four-play? Did he suck your breast? Did he give you head?" she quickly asked.

"How can we switch positions after only ten pumps? Should it have been more than ten pumps?" I ignorantly asked.

After the conversation, we both realized he had bullshit dick. He was lazy, arrogant, and inexperienced himself. It didn't matter because I didn't like sex, all that pain for no gain. Fuck that! I should have questioned why Honey asked me all those questions about our sex positions instead of asking me if was I okay? I was only 14 years old. My mind went back to the question, *how the fuck did he get in the house anyway?*

I felt obligated to continue talking to Enrique because he was my first, and I was physically attracted to him. I wanted to try sex again without the fear, and maybe it would be better if I was more relaxed. NOPE! It wasn't. It was still bullshit, dick! I didn't know at the time that he was lacking because my vagina was tight and fresh. Any penis would hurt me.

After the second time I had sex with him, I decided I didn't like sex. I didn't blame him; I assumed I was the issue. I started liking his mean ass, but it was just a little girl's fantasy lust. The second guy I had sex with fucked like a rabbit. His penis was super tiny, yet he fucked as if he was tearing something up. I only felt it because it was only my third time having sex. I concluded sex was bullshit and overrated. I kept my girl to myself for a while. I went back to the virgin me, the girl who talks shit but didn't give up any goodies.

CHAPTER 20

AT HONEY'S IT AIN'T TOO SWEET

My father and I argued more and more. He was stressed, and I was tired of living like a caged animal. My father was raising me the way a typical teenager should be raised. Not only was I not a normal teenager, but I was also far beyond my years. I needed mental help for all the pain I encountered. There was no way my father could understand how truly damaged I was. More than anything, I wanted his trust. Trust is something I took for granted when I lived with my mother.

So, here's where there is no common ground between teenagers and parents. Trust matters! If you raise a teenager too strict, it makes them think they are missing something. If you give them a little freedom, they will know they are not missing anything. They will have no interest in looking for attention in the wrong places. I didn't lack attention by any means, but I lacked freedom. Love wasn't our issue, but trust was. I was my father's entire heart, and everyone knew that. Well, not his whole heart, I did share his heart with my brothers, but I was the only girl and his oldest child.

My brothers and I had a mutual understanding. I'm the fucking boss, and that's it! They knew to respect me because they knew I would kill anyone for them without a second thought. They were my babies. They looked at me for guidance because I was the oldest. I had a beautiful relationship with all 4 of them. Desmond Jr was the second oldest, so it was just us two for a while. Cameo was next in age. Desmond Jr enjoyed being so bossy. I let him take the lead with Cameo. Mario and I had our relationship when I lived at Mary's house. Lastly, we have Clarence, who I was able to bond with from birth. So those are my brothers.

Pops and I got into an argument, and he said I couldn't go to Honey's house anymore. As a parent, that was the right decision; however, as a child, that decision crushed me. It made me spiteful. How dare he be a father and tell me I couldn't be a little pothead slut? The nerve of him to actually care. I couldn't see things his way. All I could see were my desires and my new teenage attitude. I enforced my pain on the people I loved. All the death was driving me insane, plus I missed the hell out of my mother.

I always smoked my father's joints that he left in the ashtrays. After I smoked them, I dumped the ashtray. Jen was known for cleaning and dumping his ashtray. That way, he would think she dumped it, instead of thinking I smoked it. They fussed a lot about that. I didn't do it intentionally to start an argument between the two of them. I did it to get high. Marijuana uses a part of your brain you rarely use. I needed to use that part of my brain as much as possible, so I smoked.

I loved Jen, and she tried to be patient with my father and me, but I'm sure it was hard for her. I sometimes gave her a hard way to go, not to be mean, but simply because she wasn't my Queen. I truly cared for Jen and my new baby brother Clarence, but I didn't know how to show it. I was just ready to go; it wasn't personal. I had enough. I was getting depressed, angry, and miserable. All the things my perky personality wasn't. I called my mother.

"Ma, can you come to get me? I'm miserable and sad in this house," I cried.

"Baby, I don't have a place for you to stay here where I'm at. Do you want to go to Aunt Shelby's?" she asked.

"No. I don't want to be a burden on Aunt Shelby. Let me click over and call Honey," I suggested.

We called Honey, and she said I could come live with her. My mother said she would get a ride and get me. I immediately started packing. I quietly ran up and down the steps getting trash bags to put my stuff in. I felt like shit the entire time. I knew leaving this way would break my father's heart. It was tearing me up inside, but if we had any chance to have a good relationship in the future, I would have to leave now. I packed fast and sloppy. Maybe an hour later, my mother was at the door. I quietly came to the top of the steps to listen. My father answered the door.

"Hey, what are you doing here this time of night?" he asked my mother.

"I'm here to get Sunni Desmond," my mother boldly replied.

"What?" he angrily asked. My father called me downstairs.

"I'm Coming," I nervously yelled down the steps.

"What the fuck is your mother talking about?" he asked me before I could even reach the bottom step.

"Daddy, I'm sorry, but I have to get out of here!"

"She's not going anywhere!" he yelled to my mother before he slammed the door in her face.

"Well I will have to call the police Desmond because I want my daughter," my mother yelled through the door.

My mother would never call the police for anything, so this was extreme. My father NEVER called the law either and wouldn't want them at his house. I felt worse now. I started to call the whole thing off and just take the punishment. Before I could get the balls to tell my mom just to leave me, the police were there banging on the door within 5 minutes of the argument starting. They both pleaded their cases to the officers. My father lied about some fake custody papers that didn't exist. After it was all said and done, I was able to leave with my mother. The look in my father's eyes as I walked out the door broke my heart into a million pieces, but he felt the ultimate heartbreak. He felt betrayed. My father said the most crucial statement that forever changed my life.

"You will be pregnant by the time you are 16!"

That hurt me! I knew he was hurt, but that still was a low blow. What my father didn't know is that I would prove him wrong. I would use extra protection, and I would even hide from raw dick if I had to. I would use four birth control methods. As a matter of fact, maybe I wouldn't have sex at all since it wasn't that good, anyway. What I knew was, no way would I allow myself to be pregnant at 16. That statement was exactly what my father needed to say to me. It was a blessing from God. It helped me make better decisions and constantly gave me a reason to do that much better. It stopped me from being a statistically lost pregnant teenager. I would prove him wrong at all costs, and in return, he saved my life.

Visiting Honey on the occasional weekend was fun, but things often change when you live with a person. I don't care who it is. Honey's mother, Liz, lived a few houses over. I always had a special love for Honey's mother. Liz worked for the school system and would sometimes walk me to school when I was younger. The first day I moved in, I put all my Victoria's Secret perfume, lotion, and body wash around the bathroom. My nephew instantly dumped everything out and put lotion all over the floor. Not only was I pissed, but I had to clean it up.

"Sunni, you know they are kids, right? They will do stuff!" Honey said.

"Yeah, I know, but he knows better!" I barked.

I knew she was right about them being kids, but I didn't want to hear that at that time. Them darn kids were getting into everything. I went from having my own room to sharing a room with two little boys because I wanted to be so grown. I liked kids to hug, kiss, squeeze their cheeks, chase, and tickle them, but it was always a relief to give them back to their mothers. I didn't just feel this way about my niece and nephews, I felt this way about all kids. It wasn't personal.

We went into another court in O'Donnell Heights to hang out. The court that Honey lived in was boring, and I liked that. We could have fun somewhere else, but it was mostly quiet in the part we lived in. We sometimes partied at this slut house name Terry. Yes, I could've called her something else besides slut, but honestly, there was no other name for her but slut. She slept with everyone. Perkins had some freaks, but this girl seriously had daddy issues. She was tall, big-boned, and unattractive.

Terry had the funhouse everyone would visit to smoke, drink or just get out of the cold. I once walked into her living room, and she was on her knees giving a guy a blow job. I walked in blindly, looking for Honey. Terry saw me come in and looked up but didn't stop sucking. I felt embarrassed for some reason. I don't know why? *Shit, I wasn't the one on my knees sucking dick for free.* Maybe I was embarrassed for her. She slowly took the guy's dick out of her mouth and yelled, "Shut the door!" I expected her to scream, "Get out!" Instead, she just wanted me to shut her front door. I felt weird. I thought, *hmm. Maybe I should just walk back outside.* To be honest, I was curious, and I wanted to see the guy get his dick sucked, and since her slut ass didn't kick me out, I figured why not watch?

So, she sucked on. During this time, I had no interest in putting anything in my mouth besides food. The Devil ruined that desire. Having sex here and there was one thing but putting someone's penis in my mouth was no interest of mine at my young age. I watched her gag and intensely suck his man piece. He tried to stand firm, but I watched him get weak. His eyes rolled in the back of his head, and his knees buckled. She sucked deeper and deeper.

"Damn Terry, you about to make me cum, girl," the guy moaned.

"Uhmmm," Terry moaned.

Terry sucked faster, and then she started using her hands to slowly stroke up and down. At this time, the guy was barely standing, he was getting weaker, and his man piece got harder. He then grabbed her head and jammed his dick down her throat with much force. She gagged, and when he released her for air, his dick was covered in spit.

"Don't stop sucking, hmm, don't stop," the guy demanded.

"Hhmm," she moaned and gagged. She sucked faster and more aggressively.

"Oh shit, I'm cumming. Swallow all these babies Bitch!" he yelled. He came in her mouth, and like the dumb slut she was, she swallowed all his ghetto-ass babies.

"Thanks, Boo. I'll see you later, hear," he said as he wiped the sweat off his forehead and pulled up his pants.

"Cool," Terry replied.

I thought, *what the fuck did I just see?* My panties were super wet, and my girl was tingling. Watching another person get satisfied was such a turn-on. I felt dirty. The moment the act was over, I was disgusted with myself for staying to watch the sexual encounter. Terry looked at me with a grin on her face.

"Did you like that?" Terry asked.

"Girl, I'm just looking for Honey!" I replied.

"Yeah, ok, but that didn't stop you from watching. Anyway, Honey is not here."

I didn't know what to say nor did I know why the hell I stayed and watched. Maybe I watched because I secretly wanted to see him get pleased, or perhaps I was curious about oral sex. Either way, she was a slut, and now that she was done, it was time for me to go. She bit a piece of chicken that was on the table. I awkwardly walked out the front door. I thought, *damn, she could at least go brush her teeth before putting anything else in her mouth.* I mumbled "Nutty Mouth" under my breath. I couldn't wait to tell Honey what I had just seen, but I couldn't find her anywhere. I ran into Enrique, and I smiled.

"What are you doing down here?" Enrique asked.

"Looking for Honey!"

"Oh, I saw her by her house a few minutes ago," he replied.

"Thanks, Babe," I proceeded to walk away.

"Damn, that's all?" he asked in an offended tone.

"I'll talk to you later," I said to ease his pride. I kind of liked Enrique's rude ass. I think it was just because he was my first.

I still played hard to get, but I didn't want him sexually. I got back closer to the house. I saw Honey's mother running around with a bat, and Honey was chasing her.

"Ma, come on. Get in the house. Come on!" Honey said to her mother.

"No! They are coming!" Liz yelled.

"What happened?" I asked while panting from being out of breath. I ran up to them because I saw Liz with the bat, so I figured it was an issue. If someone touched Liz, it was about to be war.

"She is sick. Please help me get her in the house," Honey said with sad eyes. I was so confused and didn't understand.

"They are coming. The army men are coming, watch that gorilla, I'm a fuck that gorilla up with this bat!" Liz continued to yell out random thoughts.

"Liz baby, you have to calm down. Come on, let's go in the house," I said as I softly grabbed her arm.

"I don't like you. Why are you here anyway? You want to use my daughter and take my grandkids from us!" Liz said as she aggressively snatched her arm away.

"She doesn't mean that Sunni, she is sick," Honey implied after seeing the hurt look on my face.

Although she had a mental episode, her words hurt. It felt like a knife slowly going into my back. This was the beginning of many nights chasing Liz. She was rapidly losing her mental stability, and it was sad. I loved her, and it hurt to see her mind go.

On top of that, she became mean and angry. Honey got her on medication, and we took turns watching her. I would do one shift, and Honey and her brother would do another. Honey's brother eventually came to move in with her, but we still had to take shifts. I didn't want to admit it out loud, but I missed the hell out of my father. I loved Honey, Liz, and the kids, but I loved my father too. I missed the simple days of just going to school, having my own room, and not being bothered if I didn't want to. This wasn't personal to Honey, but I missed stability. I would've never said it out loud, I had too much pride. Truth being, I wanted to run into my daddy's arms, beg for forgiveness, and cry.

CHAPTER 21

MONEY, DRUGS, AND A DEAD RAT

Some time went by, and we moved out of O'Donnell Heights and back into the city. The house was located on a dead-end block named Curly street. This was a new area, with new rules, and new people. The house had three bedrooms. There was a little room in the basement that Honey allowed me to sleep in. I was happy to have my own space. I didn't care the room was in the basement. I had no money, no decent clothes, or anything to keep myself up. Honey tried to help me as long as she could, but now it was time for school to start again, and I had no money for school clothes, yet again. No way was I beginning another school year looking like a bum. I needed an entirely new wardrobe.

What are my options? Get money from guys or get a job? I was only 16, and in most jobs, you had to be at least 18 unless it was a summer youth program or McDonald's. I wanted to make money fast, and being broke was getting old. So, I decided to make money both ways. Any guy who liked me would have to give me money or fuck them. I couldn't afford to be in a guy's face broke. The only problem with this plan was I didn't want to have sex with these guys. I only wanted their money. I applied for a job where the Mexicans worked. I didn't have to show any identification, so I pretended to be 18.

I worked at "Ann's House of Nuts." It was my first real job, and it paid $10 an hour. That's $80 a day before taxes of course. I got paid every week. A van picked us up and took us to the warehouse where we made trail mix. So, I had the job covered, but it wasn't guaranteed work because it was through a temp agency. Plus, the Hispanics ran that joint, so they got first picks. The Puerto Rican guy who worked at the front desk liked me, so he made sure I got on the van when he could. Money became an addiction for me. It allowed me to get the things I wanted. Mostly, I wanted to live on my own.

I ran into a guy named Don whom Honey and I knew from O'Donnell Heights. He had a big nose with Hazel eyes, and he talked a lot of shit. He was kind of cute but not my type. He was all over me, flirting and being annoying. He offered to buy us some drinks. I declined. Honey asked for a 40 oz. of Colt 45. Honey loved beer. I despised beer because I didn't like the smell or taste. I never tasted piss, but I imagined beer tasted similar to that. Don walked back on our block with us after the bar run. We talked the entire walk back.

"What's up, though?" Don asked for the millionth time.

"Why you keep saying that? What are you asking for?" I asked bluntly.

"I'm trying to fuck for real," he boldly responded.

For a split second, I was insulted. I respected his honesty, but I wasn't that girl you say that to. I wasn't fast. I was many things, but fast I wasn't. I treasured my girl. I didn't just give her away. I talked to many guys who gave me money without me giving them sex. They gave it to me because they had it and they liked me. They would eventually get bored and want pussy, and I usually would cut their asses off. Don, however, came straight out the gate asking for my girl.

"And why would I just give you some pussy? Because I ran into you on the street? Because you have hazel eyes? Oh, I know, just because you have a dick? Is that it?" I asked in a defensive tone.

"Calm down, Babe, I'm not trying to beef with you!" he replied smoothly as if he was diffusing the situation.

"Ok, nice seeing you again," I quickly said. I proceeded to walk away.

"I'm sorry pretty lady, I always thought you were pretty, and I love to look at your lips," he said as he walked up behind me.

"My lips?" I slightly smiled. I knew I had attractive lips.

"For real, I want you. What will it take?" Don continued to ask.

"$300, then you can have me," I regrettably said before I could catch my mouth from flapping. I immediately thought, *oh shit, why did I say that?*

"Damn, that's steep, Babe," he replied.

"Ok then, BYE BYE!" I said in a sarcastic but relieved tone. I was so relieved he said that was too much, I was off the hook, and my girl was safe.

"I can give you $200," he offered with a serious facial expression.

"Nah, $250," I quickly responded. I laughed to myself as if it was a joke that we were negotiating my girl. Then I thought *$250 would help out with new school clothes, and he was young and kind of cute, so what the hell.*

"$250, ok bet!" he said, snapping me out of my thoughts.

"Give me the money first!" I demanded. I thought, *Did I just sell my girl? Damn, I sold my girl for $250.* I felt weird as we walked to my room to seal the deal. He only gave me $220.

"Nope, give me what we discussed," I said with my hand out as I waited for the rest of the money.

He then handed me the other $30. I put the money up in the back of the basement, where I hid all my money. He proceeded to get undressed. Soon as I entered the bedroom, he threw me on the bed. It instantly turned me on. He bit my nipple softly. I didn't like the biting but went along with it. He then put his fingers in my girl, pulled it out, and licked them as if it was his last meal. He said this pussy tastes good too. I can't wait. He removed the rest of his clothes. He slowly kissed my nipples, then my naval. He went in between my thighs and kissed each thigh with soft, slow kisses. He kissed my girl from side to side. My mind was exploding.

He then licked my clitoris softly but with some aggression. It felt so good. It was my first time getting real four-play. It was my first time getting oral sex, period. He used his top lip to play with my clitoris and placed his tongue inside my girl. I thought, *what the fuck, this feels amazing! Maybe I should sell pussy more often. The free sex was horrible, Ok Sunni focus.* My mind was now back on the feeling, and I felt my juices and his spit running down my ass. That turned me on more. The feeling was getting intense, and he began to suck my clitoris instead of licking it. I realized I enjoyed the sucking more, so I grabbed his head so he would know not to stop.

"Hmmm," I moaned softly.

"Damn, this pussy tastes good. I could eat this shit all night," he mumbled.

At that very moment, I had my first-ever orgasm. It felt so good. I almost kissed him and said thank you or told him I loved him. My mind was tripping. I thought, *now I know why these women act crazy about sex. Shit, I've been missing out.* At that very moment, I would have loved nothing more but to go to sleep; however, I still had to give him some pussy. After all, he did pay for it. My body was so relaxed. I didn't want to move. He came up to my face and tried to enter my palace of juices. I stopped him dead in his tracks.

"Boy, where is the condom?" I asked.

"I don't have nothing. I'm clean. Come on, let me feel that pussy," Don pleaded.

"I don't care if you are clean. You still need to use a condom," I demanded. As if I was going to believe his ass, and he just paid for some pussy. He was agitated, but he put the condom on. It turned me off that he didn't want to use one. He had an average size penis, but it was fat. It hurt going in. He was the 3rd guy I had been with sexually. He kept pumping, and then he would stop.

"What's wrong? Why you keep stopping?" I asked

"Nothing is wrong. I don't want to cum yet, so I was holding my nut back."

He aggressively flipped me over and pounded me from the back. Now I was in pain and pleasure. He stopped again, but this time he pulled his penis out. I didn't ask why; he put it back in and pounded away. It felt so much better, and I became so much wetter. Once he released, he fell heavily on the bed. He didn't leave right away or rapidly get dressed. We lay there for a while.

"Real talk, I always liked you Sunni, but you were dealing with Enrique, so I never pressed up on you, but I always liked you," he said.

"Well, I never liked you!" I jokingly responded. We both laughed, but it was the truth. We lay and smoked a blunt. He left, and I fell into a deep sleep.

The next morning, I went straight to the shower. I was so upset I fell asleep without washing my ass. I guess the orgasm just wore me out. Plus, the tub was on the third floor, and after a good orgasm, that was a long walk. I got to the bathroom, sat on the toilet, and smelled this horrible, foul, disgusting odor. *What the fuck? That can't be me.* I hopped in the shower and disregarded the smell. I went to work, and when I went to use the bathroom again, I smelled like a dead rat. It was me! I panicked. I thought, *did that bitch cum in me, and his stinking nut is running out? What the fuck is that smell? No, he couldn't have released in me. We used a condom. What kind of condom? What went wrong?*

I was scared to tell Honey, but I had no choice because the smell was still there when I woke up the next day. I tried everything, a hot bath, a douche, scrubbing inside my girl, but nothing helped. The odor was so foul. I was so confused, and I replayed that night in my mind over and over again and couldn't figure out why my girl had that disgusting odor. On the third day, when I couldn't take the smell anymore, I told Honey.

"My girl smells like death," I said to Honey and lowered my head.

"What?" she laughed.

"It's not funny! Don did something to my girl, and now she smells like a dead rat!" I cried.

"Calm down, girl, tell me what happened," she snickered.

I broke down all the details of our sexual encounter. We both concluded that he snuck the condom off when he was hitting from the back. I had my first STD from my 3rd dick. The Bitch burned me! When I came from the clinic with some pills, I wanted to kill that dirty dick Bitch. I caught a cab out to O'Donnell Heights to look for him. I had a knife, a burning pussy, a bottle of antibiotics, and a lot of heart. Luckily for him, he was nowhere to be found. Yeah, I hated sex. It was always some shit with it. My first orgasm had to come with a clinic visit. Fuck sex.

I decided to just sell or hold drugs for money instead of selling my girl. My first-time holding drugs (cocaine) for the boy Josh was not what I expected. Josh worked at a Dentist's office, and he wore scrubs every day. I felt comfortable working with him because he wasn't a full-time drug dealer. He had a 9-5 job. We sat on the girl Tesa's steps; she lived across from me on Curly Street. I had a purse with three sections, two zippers on the side and one in the middle. I had all the drugs in the middle. Our drug agreement was I would be his lookout, his drug holder, and for every ten pills that he sold, I got $20. I was outside all day anyway, so no biggie, right? WRONG! The plan was only to sell drugs on the weekend. He made his first two sales like nothing. One woman walked up, and she was thin and slinky with very ashy skin.

"Hey handsome, let me get 2 for $16, Boo," the frail woman asked.

"No. I can't do it today," Josh humbly replied.

"Come on, you not going to let me go for $4? I'll bring it back later," she begged.

"No, just buy one. You too short, Mama," Josh said sternly.

She negotiated for another 10 minutes, and she somehow came up with another $2. Josh gave in and took the $18 just to get rid of her. A white man pulled up in a beat-up Toyota. He wanted ten pills of cocaine. I gave Josh 10 pills, and he sold them to him and got the straight $100. Now I have made my first $20 bucks in less than 20 minutes. I thought, *oh hell yeah, this is fast money. I can do this.* Ten minutes later, the police sped down the block and double-parked their cars. I saw them coming seconds before they got there. I immediately took the purse off and put it on the steps. It was no time to get rid of the purse or run. The cops quickly jumped out of their cars.

"Where are the drugs?" they asked.

"Man, we ain't doing shit out here," a random neighborhood guy yelled. I said nothing. Josh said nothing, but he looked at me with fear in his eyes. I guess he was wondering if would I snitch. The cops checked him and threw him on the ground. One cop walked over to check me for drugs.

"I don't have nothing, and I want a woman cop to check me," I stated.

"Do you have any weapons or sharp objects?" he asked as he proceeded to check me anyway.

"Whose purse is this?" another cop questioned. Everyone outside looked at me. I thought, *Fuck! Fuck! Fuck! Shit! What am I going to do? God, please help me.*

"I said whose purse is this?" the cop questioned again, looking in my direction.

"It's mine," I said in a harsh voice.

He opened the purse. My heart dropped. My heart was beating so fast. I started to sweat uncontrollably under my armpits. I concentrated on my plan for when he found the drugs. What would I say? Would I cry? Nah, that crying shit doesn't work with the police. The cop opened the left side and searched and searched.

"You are wasting your time. I'm a young schoolgirl. I'm not doing anything," I blurted out. My nerves were getting the best of me.

"Shut up!" he demanded. He looked at the right side of the purse and searched and searched. He found nothing. He threw my purse on the ground.

"Let them go," he told the other cops as we sat on the curb anxiously waiting.

I remained cool. As soon as they left, I breathed again. I yelled, "THANK YOU, GOD! THANK YOU, GOD! THANK

YOU, GOD!" They never checked the middle zipper; it was hidden, which is why I chose that purse to hold the drugs.

"What the fuck. How didn't they find it? I respect you, Yo. You handled that shit like a real Bitch," Josh said with excitement and relief.

"Fuck you! I don't want to be a real Bitch! I almost fucked up my life in 20 minutes. I'm trying to be something one day. Take your pills, give me $50, and we are done!" I replied. He gave me the money and a freshly rolled blunt so I could calm my nerves. After I smoked, the tension and fear went away.

"I'm out of the drug game," I joked.

Everyone laughed. God has a way of showing you what he wants from you, and he showed me in 20 minutes. I took that as a sign he didn't want me selling or holding drugs. My first-time selling pussy, I got burnt. My first-time selling drugs, I almost got burnt. Fuck that. I came to the conclusion I needed to make money another way.

CHAPTER 22

ON MY OWN

I'm almost 17 now. I've been saving my money from working. I found a new job through a temp agency where I lied about my age again. I had to quit every job I got when summer ended because I was determined to finish school. This particular job I was working had a graveyard shift, so I didn't have to quit. I worked at night and went to school during the day. I was so exhausted. I fell asleep everywhere, on the bus, at a restaurant, and even on the toilet. My new goal was to get rest instead of hanging out. 40 hours at work and 40 hours at school plus travel time was my new schedule. I saved almost every check. Now I was learning how to be a go-getter!

Honey allowed me to keep most of my money so I could move out. I loved Honey, but I wanted to move because she had another child and I felt I was in the way. I was also ready to make up my own rules and do things my way. Honey was my big sister from another mother, and all of our craziness just lead to a stronger bond between us. From the first time I saw her as a little girl sitting on the steps, I loved her. I was sad to be moving out but excited to be on my own.

I talked to my Queen every day on the phone, and she was getting herself together. That made me super happy. No matter what was going on with my mother and me, we never lost our bond. We were connected emotionally. If something was wrong with my mother, I could feel it. Nothing could come between us, no matter where I lived or what challenges we had to face. Our love was strong! I knew she did the best she could do with the cards life dealt her. As I got older, I understood how shitty life could be, and sometimes it was hard to fight against your environment. My Queen gave me the best gift a mother could ever give a child, and that was LOVE. No addiction or circumstances could come between our love. She would always be my best friend and the lady of my life.

During this time, I was also back in contact with my father. We talked every week. He wasn't doing so well around this time. He had gone to jail and lost his house and car. Jen and the baby left to live with her parents in Pennsylvania. When we reconnected on the phone, we talked about how we both felt years ago when I left his house, and we laughed about it.

"I have a confession, Daddy. That was me who smoked your weed out of the ashtrays. It wasn't Jen dumping it," I confessed.

"Shit, girl, you could've smoked with me if it would've helped your smart attitude," he responded.

"Daddy, now you know you wouldn't have let me smoke back then," I quickly replied.

"Yeah, you're right. But now that I know you blow when I see you, we're going to smoke a fat one together!" my father laughed.

Wow, how our relationship had changed. My strict father became my 2nd best friend. My parents were only about 16 years older than me. I had to remember things that happened in life weren't 100% their fault because they were young too. They were trying to find their own way and figure out this crazy place called life. How could I judge them or be mad with them when at the time life kicked all our asses? Either way, I was blessed because I had a beautiful relationship with the two people who bought me into this world.

I met a girl at the bus stop who told me an older guy name Rob rented rooms on Caroline Street, and I probably wouldn't have to show him any identification. I contacted Rob, and the rent was priced at $100 a week to rent a room. I went to see the room, and It was the biggest room in the 3-story house, but the floors were horrible.

I asked Rob if I could change the floors. He said I could, but he wouldn't discount the rent. I agreed. I moved in the next week. I became a different person. If I wanted something, I got it. I didn't like the floors, so I changed them. I became a young woman. I started to love myself again. I found my strengths in the process of finding myself. I called my father to come check out my first place.

"Daddy, can you lay some carpet for me? This floor is a mess. I'll pay you," I asked.

"Of course, baby girl, I'll come. Don't you ever offer to pay me. That's insulting," he barked.

"Sorry, Daddy. I wasn't trying to offend you. I just know it's hard work. That's all," I said apologetically.

This day will forever be a memory in my mind. This is the day I realized I had a father that would do anything for me. I reflected on how if I called him, he always came. This was the moment that explained why I expected so much from men. Why I was stingy with my girl or why I expected money from men. It's because, unlike many young girls in Baltimore, I had a father that loved me. He gave me all the money I needed, he gave me all the love I needed, and when I called, he came. So, that is what I yearned for from a man. It all started making sense.

My father came over. He had to catch two buses with heavy carpet equipment. I had never known my father not to have a car, so that told me he wasn't doing too good. We caught a hack (fake cab) to find the carpet, and he spent the entire day with me. We smoked, ate, laughed, and laid the carpet together. This was a good day in my memory. It literally changed my life. When he went to leave, I cried. I watched him walk up the street with his heavy equipment to catch the bus. I begged him to let me pay for a cab. Like the man he was, he declined.

"I'm good, baby girl, I'm a man!" were the exact words he yelled out.

Those words spoke volumes. A man does what he must do without being a burden to a woman. I made my mind up that day that I would never allow a man to become my burden. I wanted love from a mate, but I also wanted stability. I was not in the mindset to raise someone's son. At the time it felt like a regular day, but as time went on I realized that day set the standards of what I required to be loved. My love language was different because I had been through so much. A quick fuck and some sweet words weren't going to do it for me.

I finally had a better-paying job at a good company in Hunt Valley. The only problem was, I didn't want to quit the job when the summer was over, but they only had the day shift. So, school or work? NOPE! Letting go of either, was not an option, I needed both. I knew I needed help on how to keep both, so I talked to God because I finally realized I was on this journey with him. I decided to speak to the counselor at my high school. Her name was Mrs. Smith. I took a day off from work and caught two buses to the high school to put this plan into action. I waited 30 minutes and finally, Mrs. Smith called me into her office. I walked in and wasted no time getting to the point.

"Hi, my name is Sunni Connor. I'm going to the 12th grade. I have a job and my own place to live. I refuse to be a high school dropout. Can you help me?" I asked.

"Slow down. First, why are you living on your own as a minor? Second, what do you need help with?" Mrs. Smith asked.

"Never mind," I said. I started to walk out. I didn't want her to call child protective service on me for being a minor living without an adult.

"Wait, I can help you," she yelled.

"You probably can't help me," I said as I considered the option to keep walking but then I remembered I talked to God about this, so maybe she could help. This was not my problem because I gave this one to God.

"Come back and tell me what you need help with," she replied.

"Listen, I had a rough life! I don't want sympathy. I want to finish school at night to keep my day job to support myself and not become another statistic. I have all my credits, so I technically just need 12th-grade English, 12th-grade math, and Spanish 2. All of these classes are provided at night. Can I finish high school at night school?" I asked as I vented and explained.

Mrs. Smith got quiet. She looked into my eyes; then she looked away. "No one has ever dropped day school only to attend night school. I'm sorry, Sunni, but night school is only for kids who failed the classes the first time, and according to the law, all kids must go to school in the daytime during regular school hours."

"Thanks for your time," I said in a defeated tone. I felt disappointed. I felt like give me a fucking break already. I'm really trying to do right. For once, can someone help me out?

"Sorry I couldn't give you more assistance," she stated with sympathy. I walked out, then for some strange reason, Martin Luther King Jr. popped into my head, and I decided not to give up. I turned back to her and closed the door.

"There is a first time for everything. Someone always had to be the first to do something. Can you reach out to the school board on North Avenue and see if it's possible since, by law, I only need these three credits to graduate?" I asked persistently.

She was impressed that I was persistent. She suggested I write a letter to the school board director, and she would try to help me. I sat there and wrote a letter pouring my heart out, telling my story, and begging for an opportunity to finish school. Mrs. Smith called me three weeks later and said the school board approved my request and I would be the first-ever student in Baltimore city to drop daytime school and finish high school at night.

Mrs. Smith said my letter touched the school board director, and they believed in me, so they would make an exception for me to reach my goals. I screamed in her ear and cried with joy. This was the moment I knew I was different; this was the moment I knew I could create change, but I was too immature to understand how to use this power. The power of God and the power of determination is all I would need to make it. If only I could see that!

CHAPTER 23

THANKS FOR BITING MY SANDWICH

This was a good day in my life. I got a fantastic phone call from my Queen. She said she was coming over to my house and she had something to show me. When I opened the door, I saw the most beautiful, clear-skinned, long hair and bright-eyed woman I have ever seen. It was my Queen. She had to show me how she cleaned herself up. I knew she was getting help, but I didn't understand the feeling I would feel to see her be her old self again. Her thick hair was in a neat wrap style, her nails were professionally done, her makeup was perfect, her skin was flawless, and she had on the cutest jean outfit. I ran into my mother's arms.

"Ma, you look so good, and I am so proud of you. I know how hard it was for you to turn your life around," I softly cried.

"Thanks for never giving up on me, Sunni. I love you."

"I know you wanted to do it for me, but you had to do it for yourself."

"I always said I would get myself together before I had grandkids. Sunni, I had reached my weakest point ever, and I called out to God and told him I would do whatever I had to do to get out of that dark place I was in," she cried.

We hugged in the doorway for at least three minutes. Talking to my mother over the phone and hearing her voice was one thing but seeing her in person was pure bliss. My mother took her sobriety seriously. She went to NA meetings daily, and she surrounded herself with only positive people. She said she only made it out of that lifestyle by praying and having support from our family. My mother never touched another drug a day in her life. Let me repeat that! My Queen NEVER touched another drug a day in her life. My mother was back! Today was a good day (in my Ice Cube voice).

About two weeks later, I caught a hack from night school to go home because I didn't feel like catching the bus. I worked earlier that day, skipped lunch, got off, and went straight to night school. I was super hungry. I asked the hack to drop me off at the gas station on North Ave; they had just opened a new Subway Restaurant. I figured I would eat, then walk the rest of the way home. Of course, that would be too simple for my complicated life.

I went into the Subway and ordered my food. I took my sandwich and sat it on the table while I went to get my juice from the fountain machine. When I returned to the table someone had bit my sandwich. I mean a big nasty, sloppy, and spitty bite. I instantly felt disrespected.

"Who the fuck bit my sandwich?" I yelled through the Subway restaurant like a maniac. Everyone looked up at me.

"I don't know why you keep looking at me. I didn't bite your damn sandwich," a random girl responded.

"Then why are you talking?" I asked the random girl. My level of anger and hunger was getting the best of me. When

I'm hungry, I'M NUTZ! I hadn't eaten that entire day, so I was losing it.

"Girl, whatever," the random girl responded. I searched the store and saw a man chewing, but he had no food or bags.

"Did you bite my fucking sandwich?" I asked the man with anger.

"You better get the fuck out of my face!" the guy barked back.

Before I could say another word, a nicely dressed guy stepped in. He was older, in his late 20s or early 30s. He had brown caramel skin, and light brown eyes but not light like hazel eyes but light enough to notice. He was thick with a bald head. He had swag and a strong presence. He spoke with authority and demanded attention with the tone of his voice. His eyes showed strength, and only a fool would think he was to be played with. His energy was dominant.

"You better calm the fuck down, don't talk to a female like that!" the nicely dressed guy said with force.

"I'm sorry main man. My bad, Yo. I don't want no trouble," the sandwich biter said in a punk-ass voice.

"Well Bitch, if you didn't want no trouble, you shouldn't go around biting people's sandwiches," I barked. The guy left. I started to walk behind him, but I decided to let it go. The nicely dressed guy came over to me.

"Little mama, you have got to calm down. You hungry as shit, huh?" he asked with a smile.

We both laughed. I was hungry, and now I was embarrassed because I made such a scene about a damn sandwich. I hate to feel disrespected. It took me back to a place of childhood pain. It wasn't the bite that bothered me as much as the disrespect.

"What's your name, sandwich saver?" I asked.

"I'm Row," he said with confidence.

"Nice to meet you, Row. Now, you might as well buy me a sandwich after all this!" I suggested.

"Oh, you definitely get a sandwich on me. You look hungry as shit, like you're about to bite somebody," he joked.

"Be careful. I might just bite your ass," I said in a flirtatious tone.

We sat and ate our food. It was only three tables in the Subway. After some time, I realized we had been there for hours. We talked about our entire lives in such a short time. He told me he had a daughter named Sandy, and she was so bright. He showed me a picture of her, and she was for sure a cutie. I told him I just moved into the area not too long ago.

"What's up with the uniform?" he asked.

"I work in Hunt Valley," I responded while sipping my juice from the straw.

"So you got your own spot, and you work a full-time job?" he questioned.

"Yes. Why do you look surprised?" I asked. I was confused about where he was going with the conversation.

"Wow, that's crazy!"

"What's so crazy about me working and having my own place?" I asked.

"It's crazy because you have all that going on for yourself, and yet you can't afford a damn sandwich," he laughed. I punched him in the arm.

"Shut the hell up," I playfully barked. We both laughed. Here I am thinking I was about to get a compliment for being an independent, strong black woman, but nope he was dissing me. I liked his swag. I loved to laugh, and laughing with him made me feel good. I stood up and stretched. "Well, I need to get my ass up in the morning. This was nice," I said as I walked towards the door.

"Dag, you just eat up people's food and leave? Let me take you home," he offered.

"I don't get in cars with strangers," I responded.

"Girl, ain't nobody going to do nothing to your little feisty ass," he joked.

"Damn, this is fresh. I like your car!" I said. I got in his new Cadillac Deville, and he shut the door. I looked around at the new leather seats. I moved my chair back and forth with the electronic settings. I was impressed.

"Do you drive?" he asked.

"I have my permit, and I'm saving for a car."

"I'll buy you a car one day," he blurted out. I laughed. I thought, *ok, now you are gaming too much.* We listened to Biggie Smalls's song "Juicy" I rapped along…

"It was all a dream. I used to read Word Up! Magazine,
Salt-N-Pepa, and Heavy D up in the limousine
Hangin' pictures on my wall,
Every Saturday Rap Attack, Mr. Magic, Marley Marl
I let my tape rock 'til my tape popped
Smokin' weed in Bambu, sippin' on Private Stock."

"Look at you. First, you are a fighter, and now you are a rapper. You a real little thug, huh?" he smiled.

"Nah, I'm a good girl, I'm not ghetto, but I'm hood," I stated.

"What's the difference?" he asked.

"Ghetto is a style, a way of acting, a certain attitude, a certain way of cooking even. Hood is where you are from, so you know certain street things because you are from the hood," I explained.

"You are something else, so name some ghetto things. This is interesting."

"Ghetto is long nails that curl, only drinking Kool-Aid, only eating ramen oodles n noodles, every other word is profanity, speaking more slang than English, having your baby run around with just a pamper and no shoes, going to social services cursing out the government workers like you worked for those food stamps, and saying words like (baby farva)."

"Ok, I'm feeling you. What's hood shit then?"

"Hood is simply where you are from and what you have learned from your environment. Hood is understanding slang but not always speaking it. Hood is knowing the streets because you learned from the streets. A hood person is more about having hood knowledge but not necessarily picking up the ghetto characteristics. No judgment toward either one, but I'm not ghetto because I don't do ghetto things. I'm a normal chick who talks a normal way, but I'm from the hood," I explained.

"Is fighting over a sandwich a ghetto move or a hood move?" he sarcastically questioned.

"Here you go again with the sandwich thing. To answer your question, smart ass, it's a hood move. You know why?"

"Why?" he asked.

"Because in the hood, you learn not to disrespect others without consequences. So that was the hood me coming out because I felt disrespected. I learned that from my environment. Now, do you understand?"

"Yes, that makes perfect sense. Damn, Little Mama, you deep."

I hit his arm again because he was being sarcastic. We talked the entire ride home. He took a long way so he could keep me in the car longer. I didn't mind. He asked my age, and I lied and said I was 18. It was such an instant attraction between us. It couldn't be denied. Although he was older and I was younger, our chemistry didn't see age. It became a blessing that man took a bite out of my sandwich, or I would have never met my first real adult love. I said adult love because Chico would forever be my first love. I have now met MY grown-ass man. His name is Row, and he would forever change this Damaged little girl.

CHAPTER 24

ROW

I was so excited about meeting Row. Soon as I got home, I banged on my neighbor's door. Karen was a short lady who rented the room under me. She was older, but we clicked right away. She answered the door with a powder pink robe and a scarf wrapped around her head as if she was getting ready for bed.

"Girl, why are you banging on my door like you crazy?" Karen asked.

"You have to sit down for this one. I think I met my soulmate tonight," I screamed.

"Oh Lord, Sunni. Will I need a drink for this story?" she questioned.

"Yup. This is going to be a long one."

I told her the entire story about how we met and how I thought it was love at first sight. She said I was nuts. Karen and I became friends from venting in the hallway about the other dirty tenants. We also discussed how we were getting ripped off by the landlord. The following day, I called my mother to fill her in with all the "Row" details.

Row was attractive for sure, but my type was young, braids, slim and dark. Row was thick, bald, and older. I didn't care what he looked like because he had swag, and we had undeniable chemistry. He was a confident man; he was serious but funny. I could instantly tell I would be safe with him. He called me the day after we met and told me he could not stop thinking about me and that he wanted to take me out. I was blushing the entire phone call because I couldn't get him off my mind either. I agreed to go on a date with him, and he said he would pick me up at 8 o'clock.

I went to the Inner Harbor to go shopping at the Gallery. I grabbed a cute outfit and some accessories. I got my nails done, fixed my hair, and got super cute. When he met me, I was tired and looking rough in my work uniform. I wanted to show him I clean up very well as a baddie. He called me at 6 o'clock and told me how he couldn't wait to see me and asked where I wanted to go? I told him to surprise me. Eight o'clock came, and I called him, no answer, so I waited another half an hour and still no answer. He stood me up! I was dressed, looking cute, and had no date. I left him a voicemail cursing him out.

"You are a lame ass dude not to answer your phone, stood me up instead of being honest. I don't like your bald head, OLD ass anyway, lose my number, loser."

He called around 11 o'clock that night. I refused to answer. I thought, *who the fuck does he think he is? Old bitch, standing me up. He must be crazy.* Row continued to call nonstop. He was so persistent. Around Midnight I finally answered the phone.

"Hello," I loudly answered.

"So I'm a lame old loser, huh?" he chuckled.

"Yup. That shit you pulled was whack, and I don't get down like that. So, what do you want? I'm busy," I asked firmly.

"Come outside, please," he pleaded.

"Outside? For what? Like I said, I'm busy. I thought older guys were more mature. I see y'all old asses play games too," I said with agitation.

"Are you coming? I'll tell you what happened when you get in the car. Did you eat?" he asked, completely disregarding my slick comments.

"You don't get to make up the rules. Stand me up and think I'm just waiting around for you. As I said, I'm busy!"

I panicked. I was in a holey t-shirt with bleach stains, some ugly walk-around-the-house pants, and a silk scarf on my head. I peeked out the window and saw his car. *Shit, his crazy ass is really here.* I ran around the room, trying to find something to put on. I found a cute pair of jeans and a tank top. I ran to the shared bathroom to brush my teeth and wash my face. I was happy no one was in there. I continued to hold the phone as I rushed to get dressed.

"Damn, people make mistakes Sunni. That's fucked up. You not even going to come to the car?" he asked as he continued to plead his case.

"Shut up, stop whining and look up!" I demanded. I was at my front door, locking it with my keys. He had the biggest grin on his face when he saw me walking toward his car. I got in the car, and he instantly hugged me.

"That's why I fuck with you," he whispered in my ear as he continued to hug me.

"Yeah, whatever, don't pull that stunt again," I said, still playing tuff. Deep down inside, I was in pure bliss just being in his presence.

We ate pizza from Crazy Johns in Downtown Baltimore. It was a late-night spot with tasty pizza. It was always entertainment on the strip. After we left the chaos from the block (Downtown), we drove around talking until 5 a.m. He would randomly touch my hand or my ear. He smelled my neck and looked into my eyes whenever we stopped at a red light. He let me be the talker I was. I loved how he never interrupted me or seemed annoyed I was chatty. He seemed to love to hear what I had to say, and he valued my opinion about politics, violence, the streets, or whatever we were talking about at the moment.

"You are so beautiful. You have natural beauty, not like these made-up chicks," Row complimented.

"Thanks," I blushed. Row drove me home, and we tongue-kissed for what felt like an eternity. My panties were so wet. I squirmed around in the front seat of his car. The feeling was too intense, and I didn't want to give up my goodies on the first night. I removed my seat belt and backed away from his lips.

"Why are you leaving?" He asked.

"I have to go to work in a few hours. I'll call you later," I said in a sexy, seductive voice.

"Ok, Pretty Young Thang," he chuckled.

"Don't ever call me that corny shit!" I laughed.

"I love that feisty mouth of yours. See you later Pretty Young Thang," he repeated.

I shook my head, and he pulled off. I ran up to my room, feeling better than I'd felt in months. I was on a "Row" high. I daydreamed about him and remembered his touch and his amazing lips kissing me into wetness. I slept so peacefully for 2 hours before it was time for me to go to work. Every day Row and I were together. That's how fast it happened. I was now in love with this grown-ass man. He was my baby. I told him everything, and I didn't make any decisions without talking to him first. Not because he was a control freak but because he was my best friend. We went out for a few months, and we only kissed, but we never had sex. I confessed after the 3rd date that I was only 17 years old.

"I know I'm older than you Sunni, but I can't help how I'm drawn to you," Row said.

"I feel the same way. I feel so connected to you. Like they say, age ain't nothing but a number," I chimed in.

"Yeah, that's what they say," he agreed.

"Is that why you never tried to have sex with me?" I questioned.

"I'm not in a rush to have sex with you because I know you will be my girl. I will get that pussy whenever I want but just know once daddy put this thang on you. It's a wrap!"

I blushed super hard. This was our one and only conversation about age. It never came up again. I knew I needed a mature guy because I had been through a lot. I didn't have an immature mindset like other people my age. I was working, going to school, paying rent, and about to move into my second place. What could a 17-year-old boy do for me? Other people my age were preparing for prom, school dances, being spoiled brats, or doing something age-appropriate.

I moved into my gorgeous new place. The ceilings were high, the floors were hardwood, and it was so spacious. I moved to Mount Royal Terrace. The building was stunning; it was very historical. It was a significant upgrade from the room I rented. This was yet another proud moment in my life. I was in my second place under the age of 18, and I was doing it on my own. I started to feel like my life was finally coming together. I felt like I finally got rid of death.

Row helped me move in. He placed the boxes on the kitchen floor, and I was about to ask him a question when he picked me up by the waist. He threw everything on the counter to the floor. He aggressively pulled my shirt off and kissed my bottom lip.

"I love you, Sunni," he whispered.

"I love you too, old man," I softly said.

He smiled and kissed my chin and then my neck. He took off my bra and looked at my perfect perky breast, and smiled with anticipation. He slowly and softly kissed my nipples then he sucked them while he unbuckled my pants. He lifted me off the counter and pulled my pants down. He bit my underwear and pulled them down with his teeth until they got to my knees. I got excited, thinking he was about to suck my girl, but he came back up to my other nipple and sucked it softly. I was about to explode. I felt like I was about to cum just from him sucking my breast.

Row then kissed the middle of my stomach. He pulled his pants down and put his hand on his already hard piece of wood. I removed his hand, and I begin to jerk his dick slowly. He continued to kiss me all over. He worked his way down to my legs and kissed my calves. He kissed every inch of me. He savored my body in anticipation. We both had been waiting for this day. He came back up to my thighs and kissed all around my girl without ever kissing her. The tease was killing me. I begged, but he teased me more.

Row finally slowly and softly licked my girl. I roughly grabbed his bald head, and he started softly sucking my clitoris. His mouth was hot. It was like he knew exactly what to do. He sucked my clit a little more aggressively, and he put one finger in my girl, slowly pulling his finger in and out in a circular motion. I was now screaming and having a massive orgasm. He wiped his face and acted as if he was about to walk away like he accomplished his goal. I aggressively grabbed his arm and pulled him back towards me. I roughly inserted his penis in my overly excited wet vagina. It was the best feeling ever. He kissed my neck and deeply stroked.

"Damn, is this my pussy?" he asked as he moaned and stroked.

I didn't respond; instead, I moaned more. I was in the perfect place of agony and pleasure. He picked me up from off the counter, never removing his penis. He walked me to the bedroom with his hard hot stiff dick penetrating my G spot. I was now having multiple orgasms. We made it to the room, and he sat on the bed with his man piece still in me. I rode him like no tomorrow. I took my hands and played with his balls while I rode as if I had a destination. When I felt like he was about to cum, I would hop off his dick to make him hold it back. I put his man piece in my mouth and slowly sucked.

"Oh shit, Sunni, stop, stop, before I cum," Row moaned and pleaded.

"Beg me to stop," I whispered. I would tease him to the point he was almost there. Then I would stop and hop right back on his dick. I came again. Now I was drained and weak.

"You know you mean the world to me," he softly said.

"I love you, Row," I whispered. I softly kissed his lips and licked all my juices off his top lip.

He then flipped me over, and now I was on the bottom. He was grinding and grinding. I moaned, and I couldn't believe I was about to cum again. He softly kissed my lips and pulled his penis out, and came all over my thighs. He made love to me. My first grown man took my body to a world I didn't know existed. I never had an orgasm from a penis before, only oral sex. Not to mention I never had multiple orgasms before. He fucked up now! I was in love, and I would become a crazy bitch over this man! I mean really crazy! That's the power of the mighty penis. We took a shower together and spooned until morning. We never unpacked or did anything to the apartment.

Row was the love of my life. He had me gone. I was so in love; I got his name tattooed on my ass. By now, I had many tattoos, some professionally done and some I had done at a house tattoo party. I told him if we ever broke up, I would leave his name on my ass until someone took care of me as he did. He bought me whatever I asked for.

Row gave me an allowance, and I shopped like never before. He bought me whatever I asked for. Nothing but the best. Bags, $300 sunglasses, the dopest shoes, or whatever I wanted. I never had this kind of money in my possession before, and I loved it. The problem was it was drug money, and there is always a problem with fast money. I knew this from the streets but figured since he didn't hustle on the street corner, maybe it would be ok. I thought, *he's a boss, so since he only picks up the money, it shouldn't be too many problems.*

When I turned 18, Row surprised me with stacks of money and so many gifts. He said it was time for a car. He kept his promise he made when we first met, and he helped me buy my first car. He wanted to pay for the entire car, but I declined. I needed to feel secure and independent. I needed to feel like it was my car. So, he gave me half, and I paid the rest. Uncle Charlie drove me to Pennsylvania, where I bought a Crown Victoria from an old white woman. I was supposed to get something cute and small, but Uncle Charlie said the Crown Victoria would be reliable. It only had one owner and hardly any miles. I always listened to Uncle Charlie, so I came back to Baltimore with a big boat. When I showed Row the car, he laughed and laughed.

"Girl, what are you going to do with that big ass car?" he questioned with laughter.

"I'm a whip, that big bitch!" I responded.

We both laughed. Now, although Row spoiled me, I was sure to always keep my own money, a job, and enough money to pay my own bills. Row did the extra. As my relationship got more serious, I realized Row would lie about dumb shit. We argued about these lies. I couldn't understand why he lied so much, so I started ignoring him when I thought he was lying. That was our only issue (the lies). Our sex life was great! We had sex everywhere. We once had sex on the field on Madison Street, where the marching bands practiced. This was not a secluded area, but we didn't care. We went to the field often.

"Why do you love coming to this field?" I asked.

"It's the best place to see the stars," he responded.

"You're right. I never noticed that. So are you into astrology and stuff?" I asked.

"I won't say all that, but I know a lot about the planets. Your man low key smart," he chuckled.

Row always seemed to amaze me. He was so intelligent. He knew things that no one else knew, but he was in the streets. A lot of street guys were brilliant. They were also habitual liars. He started staying up when he came over. He couldn't fall asleep. Something was bothering him. I kept grilling him.

"Baby, what's wrong?" I questioned.

"Nothing is wrong. I already told you that," he barked.

He got so upset that I kept asking him questions. He left in the middle of the night. He came back a few hours later and apologized. He was different, and something was wrong. Whatever it was, he didn't want me to know. I started thinking maybe he was cheating. I couldn't imagine why he would cheat, but men cheat all the time. I never wanted to be that girl that says, "My man doesn't cheat." Just the thought of him touching someone else made me furious. A few days later, he came to my apartment upset and said he had to talk to me.

"I got into some beef with this dude about some money! I just wanted to put you on point. You know where the hammer at, right?" Row nervously asked.

"Yeah, I know where the gun is unless you moved it. So what happened? Fuck, I don't want you beefing," I honestly stated.

"I didn't want to worry you. We are having a sit down to squash it tomorrow, but I will kill him if I have to," Row said with no emotion.

That conversation scared me. I was from the streets, so I knew that was not good. Any kind of beef in the streets was not good. I knew I was dealing with a street guy, and things like this came with the game, but it worried me. Two days later, we sat on the end of my bed as we talked about life.

"Baby, that beef is squashed. The sit down went well," Row said in a calm tone.

"So y'all figured out the money issue?" I questioned.

"Yup. Don't worry. Of course, you always need to check your surroundings. No one is ever to be trusted. We live in a ruthless ass city."

"Who you telling. I know this city oh so well," I agreed.

I felt relieved. I was happy the beef was over. About a week later, Row was with his associate Malcolm. I was not fond of Malcolm at all. He tried to push up on me one day when Row wasn't around. I never told Row what happened out of fear Row would go off or possibly kill him. I kept it to myself, but I put Malcolm in his place. I just didn't like his slimy ass. I later found out he was a horrible person; he was actually a hitman.

It can't get much worse than that. I had three missed calls from Row. I immediately called him back.

"Boo, you good? I saw you called," I asked.

"Yup, I'm good. I'm with Malcolm about to hit the liquor store. Do you want something?" Row asked.

"I'll take some Absolut Vodka with cranberry juice. How long are you going to be?" I asked.

"Not long, babe. I promise," he responded. He called back 20 minutes later.

"I'm at the liquor store. They only have pineapple juice," he said.

"That's cool babe, I'll be waiting for you butt naked," I said, deciding not to nag. I briefly thought to myself, *his ass is always lying. He said he was at the liquor store 20 minutes ago.*

"Oh shit naked, that's what I'm............"

I heard BOOM BOOM. The phone disconnected. I thought, *what the fuck? He dropped that damn phone again.* I called back repeatedly. No answer. Now I was getting worried. I called back again, and a Chinese man answered.

"He gone, he gone," the Chinese man hollered.

"What? Did you say he's gone? He left his phone?" I asked.

"No, he die, he gone, he gone, police coming," the Chinese man hollered again.

"What the fuck you mean he died? Hello, hello!" I yelled. I paused as the phone disconnected in my ear. I dropped the phone and screamed, "NOOOO, NOOOO, please, please, please, please NOOOOOOOOOOOO."

I punched and screamed and punched and screamed. I said to myself, *no fucking way he's gone, let me go find my baby. That Chinese man could have the wrong guy.* I threw on some clothes. Since my car wasn't registered yet, I put a sign in my car window that read "stolen tags." I made it to the liquor store without getting pulled over or crashing. I saw the yellow police tape around the liquor store. I peeked in, but I couldn't see.

"Do you know the victim's name?" I asked the cop. He stood close to the store door.

"No, please back up," the cop responded.

"Is it a black male with a bald head? Please tell me," I pleaded.

"Miss, please back up. I'm sorry I can't confirm the identity of the victim," the cop said. He answered this time in a more sympathetic tone.

I didn't see any of Row's cars, so I got hopeful that maybe they had the wrong person, but maybe he was in Malcolm's car. My mind raced, and I was out of it. I saw Row's brother, and my heart dropped. Before he could say the words out of his mouth, I saw the look in his eyes, and I knew it was Row. My heart instantly broke. I fell into his brother's arms and hit his chest repeatedly.

"Why, why, why?" I sobbed.

"Sunni, I'm so sorry," he said with sympathy. He held my weak body as I slowly slid down to the ground.

The pain of losing the first man I was in love with was unbearable. I was in more pain than my heart could tolerate. I literally felt my heart breaking into a million pieces. At some point, his brother must've let me go because I found myself on the curb. There I lay in the gutter on Greenmount Avenue. I lost track of time. I could hear chatter from the nosey neighborhood people in the background.

I went to that shutdown place I went to when Uncle Tom died. I didn't speak. I couldn't speak. I became numb. Row's face kept flashing in my mind, his straight teeth, his one dimple, his smile, his bald head, his muscular arms he was so proud of after just joining Bailey's Fitness. I reminisced about all the times we shared. The first day I met him at Subway, Our first date, the late-night star watching, the first time we had sex, the moments we watched TV as he touched my ears, the showers we took together, the fun we had on my 18th birthday, the times I would kiss him while he slept peacefully, the look on his face when I showed him his name tattooed on me and how happy he was, not to mention all the many times we made love.

Yup, good Ole Row is gone! Someone blew his brains out right while we were on the phone. That BOOM BOOM I heard were gunshots. In my gut, I knew it was that slimy as Malcolm, and he knew I knew. I remember Row telling me he was at the liquor store with Malcolm. I also knew Row would never let a stranger get that close to him to blow his brains out. He was always on point. His vision was sharp, and the likelihood of him slipping was close to none. Malcolm always looked at me with a threatening look which confirmed it. I didn't care. Whenever I ran into Malcolm, I always mugged him. I would look him in the eyes to let him know that I knew he killed Row. For my safety, I couldn't tell what I knew. After all, he was a hitman.

My mother went with me to the viewing. She liked Row a lot, he often spoiled her as well but she was too sad to go to the funeral. Uncle Charlie took me to the funeral. Uncle Charlie was always like my second father and showed up whenever I needed him. We had this bond since I was a baby. Uncle Charlie stayed with me the entire day, even for the repast. Honey came to support me as well. I sat with Row's daughter Sandy at the funeral. Sandy was sad but seemed stronger than me. Sandy was so pretty and intelligent, just like her father. Row would often bring her over, and we really clicked. She was such a sweet little girl.

I was almost 19 years old and 125 pounds when Row was murdered. I grieved so hard, and it was hard to absorb the pain. I couldn't cope with the loss. I lost 15 pounds, and people had the nerve to judge me. They said things like, "have you seen Sunni? she is thin." I didn't care what they said, fuck them. I knew I had experienced death many times before, but this was different. This experience kicked my ass. I was never the same. I officially became a new person, and not in a good way. I lost another chunk of myself that I would never get back. My innocence was completely gone. I was officially a grown-ass woman with a soul of a damaged little girl.

Maybe I shouldn't love at all. When do I get to live? How many black dresses must I wear? This was my fucked-up life, my fucked-up choices, and my fucked-up destiny. Or was it my fucked-up environment? My fucked-up city, maybe? Or maybe it was the atmosphere in those fucked-up streets? Whatever it was, one thing was for sure I was a fucked up DAMAGED little girl. Or was I? Death happened to be all of our destinies, and maybe I lost more than others, but I was NOT death. I was however 18 years old and learning the most important lesson of my life which was, we enter this world with NOTHING, and the end result is we leave this world with NOTHING. So, what's in between nothing and nothing? A life worth living!

CHAPTER 25

BALTIMORE

I thought of sugar-coating this chapter. I can't sugarcoat what I said because the shit ain't sweet. The truth is bitter, and this was my harsh reality.

What is Baltimore? What does the city consist of? Is it like what people have heard? No way it's that much violence in such a small city? Baltimore is the beautiful Inner Harbor and the iconic Lexington Market. It's one of the most beautiful cities from above to fly over at night. That is the image of Baltimore. It's like a fake marriage that looks so nice, but when the couple gets home, they sleep in different rooms. Those rooms are considered to be zip codes. Depending on what zip code you live in; is what determines your marriage. Let's skip the B.S. and get right down to it.

Some may judge my life and the obstacles I had to face, but truth be told, the city of Baltimore puts you in these situations no matter where you live. I can't blame all my troubles on Baltimore because I made a few bad choices along the way. It's funny how these choices aren't an option in a different environment. Unfortunately, being surrounded by negativity without guidance allows you to fall victim to Baltimore city's pain.

Now, I'm not saying we don't have successful people from our city. Nor am I saying everyone falls victim to the circumstances. I'm not saying everyone had the damaged childhood I had, but many did, in one way or another. What do I mean by that? Many people who live in the inner city cannot honestly say they have not lost a loved one to violence. Or they don't have someone in their family who was addicted to drugs. Most of my childhood friends' parents did drugs as well.

I am saying that the odds are GREATLY against you, and you have a huge chance of becoming a product of your environment (most of the city). We are surrounded by poverty, negativity, drugs, ignorance, addicts, prostitution, drug dealers, and an abundant amount of violence. Unfortunately, this is the culture of Baltimore. Good people live here that genuinely want this city to be great. There are some decent areas with less violence, depending on your zip code. For the most part, it's what I said it is. It's a city of poverty! The school system suffers more than many would like to admit, which is a great misfortune for our new generation of Kings and Queens. I won't dare talk about the crooked politicians and how everyone has their hands in the pot of gold; when the money should go to the youth and the schools.

Every hood in Baltimore is different. The people that live in West Baltimore act utterly differently from the people who live in East Baltimore. It's funny because people from West Baltimore seem to think they are better dressed or less ghetto. NOT! It's ghetto and tacky people on both sides. Now the truth is most people from East Baltimore are scammers. They are all for themselves. It's all about what you can do for them—tit for tat.

Certain parts of West Baltimore dynamics are different because they have bigger houses, so, at some point, they come from more money vs. the row houses over East Baltimore. It's still that way. However, some parts of West Baltimore, like Pennsylvania Ave, known as "The Avenue," is in a category all by itself. It's walking death, to say the least—death from violence or death from drugs. You choose.

The same thing for the projects, O'Donnell Heights was NOTHING like Perkins, nor were the people. Cherry Hill and West Port are on their own project planet. It's almost like they are in different time zones. They have their own hood rules and their own hood mentality. It's like someone just dropped that entire community off out of a spaceship in the middle of nowhere, with no stores or no way out to even try to have a proactive life. Why would they build an entire community without good transportation and stores? Think about that for a second. It was designed for failure. It's bigger than the people. It's a poverty setup.

Yet we still managed to have some die-hard Cherry Hill people who became great success stories. If, for a split second, you think this is about race, sorry, it's not. Here's why, South Baltimore is a planet of its own as well (Wilkens Ave, Pig Town, Pratt Street, etc.) It's a lot of prostitution, poor white trash, poor mixed trash, and poor black trash. Either way, it's mainly made up of poor trash. It's a diverse community of all different races of trash. I know, I know, that may seem harsh but remember what I said at the beginning of this chapter, the shit ain't sweet.

Of course, there is always an exception to every rule. I wouldn't dare judge an entire community; I don't judge at all. I'm only speaking of the odds. I am only speaking from my perspective. This is not about bringing my city down or putting specific neighborhoods on blast. This is about the big fat elephant in the room. The Bitch name is Poverty, and she lives in other cities too. I could go on and on about each neighborhood in Baltimore, but that would be a drag.

There are those lucky people who were raised by an old-school grandmother who didn't allow her children to live the way the people lived outside. Or the mothers who went to college and raised their kids with a successful mentality. Or the father who had a traumatic experience and decided to do a better job at raising his own children. It's always an exception. The point is no matter where you live in the city of Baltimore you must be built strong to survive. Literally! You could walk outside your door and be shot. You see the body count on the news, right? (well, what the media reports, at least).

Our poor babies see nothing but destruction when they walk out of their doors. Poverty is their visual on most Baltimore city streets. They wake up to the noise. They wake up to drug addicts. They wake up to the drug dealers on the corners early in the morning instead of seeing business owners or proud people going to work. They wake up to other races (Chinese, Korean, Indian, etc.) owning stores in our neighborhoods instead of people with their skin color. Some of their fathers are dead or in jail, so they have no choice but to look up to the men in their environment.

Are ALL the men in Baltimore no good drug dealers? Of course not. We have some strong men who will die for these young kids and try their best to show them a different way of life. Some of the drug dealers/street guys are beautiful people who just got lost in their environment. Many community activists also make sure we have back-to-school supplies for the children and try to make a change behind the scenes. Some mothers do their best to raise their kids without their child's father. Unfortunately, some don't. Some are lazy and let the kids raise themselves. They would rather get a government check than work, but there's a problem with working. It doesn't pay off. Huh? Stay with me!

You make just enough money to pay your bills because the moment you make decent money, the government assistance stops, which puts these single mothers in a lower class than the lower class. That doesn't mean they shouldn't work. It just means a lot of people will still be struggling financially. A considerable percentage of the city is on government assistance, including section 8 housing vouchers. The orange food stamp card is like a black card in our city.

Yes, there are working people in Baltimore! Of course, we are part of the economy too! Some women and men work damn hard to stay out of trouble and take care of their families. Sadly, the odds are still against us. Our rent is expensive, and opportunity is limited in these poverty-stricken areas. No excuses, though. We can still be great, but we need a chance, and many of us don't get it, or we don't have a positive influence to show us how to get it. This is not a judgment of MY city; this is the truth. This is my truth!

I will offend some people or make them upset about how I have portrayed our city. That's backlash I'm ready and willing to take. I firmly stand by what I said. If you think this city is not filled with Violence, Poverty, Death, and Drugs, then write your own book called "Baltimore city is GREAT, RICH and NO ONE DIES!" (sarcastically laughing). My damage wasn't caused by my mother, father, or family. It was life! It was my environment! It was Death! We are all death. The moment we breathe life, we are already dying. I can't blame my parents for their mistakes because they had the same fucked up environment I had. They had to fight the same odds. Some battles they won and some battles they lost but they were both AMAZING PARENTS!

With all I said about Baltimore, I wouldn't have wanted to grow up anywhere else. Yeah, I said it, and I'll repeat it. I wouldn't have wanted to grow up anywhere else. This city made me brick strong, and I learned more than most humans will learn in a lifetime. This city molded me and showed me the cold truths of what life can be. It also showed me strength, courage, love, and independence. I can handle anything. I can go anywhere. I can adapt to any situation. I fear nothing. They call us the "crab city." I think the name fits our city perfectly. The vibe of the city is like crabs in a barrel. One crab tries to get out, and the rest of the crabs drag him back down. My entire life, I was that one crab trying to get out. Did I make it out? Or did this DAMAGED little girl become a DAMAGED woman? Nothing is what it seems!

TO MY FATHER

I love you, boogie. Thanks for your love and support over the years and for putting up with me and my smart mouth. You are indeed an amazing father, and you would go to no lengths to protect me. I know this journey has been challenging for you as well, and I want you to know I'm grateful. Thanks for allowing me to tell my truth. I appreciate you making me remove that earring from my nose when I was 12 years old. Thanks for staying on my case regarding school. The fact you were so hard on me about school is why I was so persistent about not giving up, and it made me determined to finish. Our bond is so strong, and the years missed are the years gained. You taught me how a man should provide and protect with no excuses. Take care of home first, and for that reason, I'm hard on these men. I thank you for all the headaches you gave me as well! All the headaches I gave you as a teenager, you happily paid me back as an adult. You taught me patience, love, and, most importantly, you taught me I can have whatever I want from this world because it was foretold. I'm so blessed God granted me the honor to be your one and only daughter. I love you, Daddy!

Love Sunni T,

TO MY READERS

Thank you for reading my life story. I appreciate the time you invested in reading my book. If I could hug you, I would. Exposing my life was the hardest and most liberating thing I've done to this day. I humbly say thanks for all your support.

This was my first ever published book and I've learned and grown tremendously as an author. I wanted the writing to be in my voice and as raw as possible to tell the story most authentically. I decided not to have this particular book re-edited because my imperfections show my growth and to this day this is still one of my top-selling books. If you felt you were in my world, that's exactly what I wanted.

The sequel to this book is called A DAMAGED WOMAN and is available at www.amazon.com or www.naturallysunni.com. If you have time please leave a review, it's how many authors are recognized. ☺

BOOKS FROM THE AUTHOR

1. Damaged little Girl: Nothing Is What It Seems (Memoir Part 1)
2. A Damaged Woman: The Sequel (Memoir Part 2)
3. Damien's Secret 1: The Truth Is Within The Eyes (Suspense Fiction)
4. Damien's Secret 2: Welcome To The Dark Side (Suspense Fiction)
5. Niña Dañada: Nada Es Lo Que Parece (Spanish Version)
6. El Secreto De Damien: Parte 1: La verdad está en los ojos (Spanish Version)
7. El Secreto De Damien: Parte 2: El lado Oscuro (Spanish version)
8. Society vs You: Play The Game Your Way! (self-help)

FOLLOW ME

IG @sunni_theauthor
FB @Sunni Connor

GIVE BACK

If you want to give back to the Prison Libraries by donating to my foundation, "Books For Time." To give a $10 donation, please visit www.naturallysunni.com/books-for-time

WHERE TO LEAVE A REVIEW

www.amazon.com
www.goodreads.com
www.barnesandnoble.com

WANT TO BOOK A SESSION WITH ME?

Vist www.naturallysunni.com/services

~ ACKNOWLEDGEMENTS ~

I want to first thank God for all my many blessings and for never leaving me in the darkness. I send thanks and love to my beautiful children Zi'yas, Terrah, and my goddaughter Peyton; they were so patient and understanding of what mommy was trying to do. They love me unconditionally, and they sacrificed being uncomfortable for my dream. They are the best kids a mother could ever ask for, and I thank God for them every day. Thanks to my parents Tonia Martin Rouzer, Dant'e Connor, and my stepfather Gregory Rouzer for supporting, understanding, caring, and providing positive encouragement.

I want to give special thanks to my Uncle Hank (Henry Connor), my second father. Your love for me has always been solid and pure. I appreciate you, Uncle Hank, and I will never forget all the many times you showed up with no complaints. Thanks to my Aunt Shell (Michelle Martin Jones), who answered whenever I called. I love you, Auntie, and thanks for loving me like one of your own children from day one. Special thanks to Veny (Carlos DeOliveira) for allowing me to vent and loving me with no stipulations. Thanks for your continued patience.

Thank you to my special editing team for the help with the first published edition. Jordache Marston, thanks for your dedicated time with all you had going on, including the startup of your own company, "TGIT mindset." I will never forget your dedication. Thanks, Tonja Mask, for being a true friend and listening to all my ideas nonstop. You also dedicated time to help with the editing process, and I will never forget your kind heart. Special thanks to my babies, Adriana Sanders, Jadyn

DeOliveira, and Laila DeOliveira, for your last-minute dedication to the editing process. You girls were very supportive, and I'm forever grateful. Thanks, Kennard Carver, for being my "Ghost Reader." Thanks for your positivity and your daily encouraging words. You believed in me and helped me stay on the path of my dreams.

Nikki (Shaniqua Singleton), you inspired me to keep going, and your excitement for my goals is exactly how a friend should act, and for that, I love you. To my best friend, Ciera Stokes, we don't talk daily, but we don't need to. We love each other unconditionally. Thanks for loving my babies and me and providing the security to know you'll always be there.

To Andrea Brown, you made my childhood a joy, and I'm so blessed God continues to grant you life. I will forever love you, Twin. To my sister Toni (Patricia Williams), you were there for me since the first day I met you. I love you, sister. To Nakia Brockington, we were once considered "New Friends," and now we are ten years strong. Thanks for never judging me and always supporting my go-getter mentality. I love you, girly.

Very special thanks to my siblings for always looking up to me. Because of you all, I made better decisions out of fear of disappointing you (Angel Connor, Cameron Connor, Marcel Connor, Clayton Connor, and Lil D). Thanks to my beautiful cousins, who I've always loved like we were siblings, Dominique Johnson, Jamal Connor, Travis Connor, Diane Frazier, Dexter Martin, Michael Clanton, Monique Scott, Jazmine Collins, Candi Ohira, and the late Davon Johnson. Thanks to all my lovely friends, family, and supporters.

To the late Barbara Rodriguez, you were my biggest fan. You believed I could move mountains. There was no idea too crazy or no career too ambitious for me to conquer. I watched you live your life effortlessly without a care in the world. The day I told you I was quitting my job, writing a book, and starting my own company, you screamed on the phone with joy. Your exact words were, "Mami, what took so long?" All your craziness was worth every minute I got to spend with you. I DID IT B !!! Continue to rest easy.

REST IN PEACE, BABIES!

I would like to take a moment to acknowledge how much these beautiful souls impacted my life. May you all rest peacefully and know I will forever love you.

Pamela W
Marcus L,
Roger C,
Edward P,
Barbara R,
Davon J,
Charisse H
Nolan M,
Tyrell R,
Theresa S,
Charles Sr M.,
Charles Jr M,
Jazmine R,
Tom W
Carlos R
Tavon S